THE HEDGEHOG
& Friends

THE HEDGEHOG & Friends

More Tales from St Tiggywinkles

Les Stocker

Drawings by Guy Troughton

Chatto & Windus

LONDON

Published in 1990 by
Chatto & Windus Ltd
20 Vauxhall Bridge Road
London SW1V 2SA

A CIP catalogue record for this book is available
from the British Library

ISBN 0 7011 3655 3

PICTURE CREDITS

Drawings © Guy Troughton;
Cartoon p. 25 © Bill Tidy;
A–Z of Garden Hazards © Thames Television plc 1988;
Photos pp. 69, 70, 82, 100, © Bucks & Herts Newspapers Ltd.

Photoset and printed in Great Britain by
Redwood Press Limited, Melksham, Wiltshire

Contents

Acknowledgements

Fortunately, more and more people are becoming aware of wild animal and bird casualties. Because of this, our workload at St Tiggywinkles has grown enormously: almost every day, evening and night is now taken up with patients. In reading *The Hedgehog & Friends* you will see how many have joined our volunteer teams. It is these fosterers, rescuers, cleaners and administration teams who give the animals the chance to live and rejoin their wild relatives. I will keep saying, 'Thanks for your help,' even though I know they don't expect gratitude, just the chance to help wildlife.

Sadly, some of our team have moved to pastures new but I would still like to acknowledge the assistance in our formative years of Russell Kilshaw and Andy Walton, neither of whom ever shirked sharing a night-call with me.

In writing this book I am, as always, indebted to Sue, my wife, and Colin, my son, for their guidance and support, and to Catherine Miller for once again ploughing through my manuscript.

Finally, I would like to thank you all for outlawing at last the bread and milk diet that has, in the past, killed so many hedgehogs.

1 Foundling and Foxes

Two brown button eyes stared petrified up at me from the cardboard box. Surely this couldn't be a fox cub. Carefully, I opened the box wider, revealing a small, frightened face with a dark black nose, a jaw hanging useless and a tongue drooping out where the teeth should have been. It wasn't a fox cub – it was a tiny dog in an appalling condition. His ears flattened as I reached in to lift him out. He shook uncontrollably, both from fear and cold, for apart from a few tufts of rufous hair on his head and feet he was completely bald. And to add to that, his bald skin was pitted with scars and sores, and set off by a completely naked stalk of a curly tail.

His miniature body just filled both my hands, and his eyes were watering – as mine were, at the state he was in. What had he been through and who had let him get into this condition and then callously dumped him by the roadside at the mercy of the traffic and the night?

Luckily, some kind people had heard his whimpering and, mistaking him for a 'mangey fox cub', had put him onto some dry towels in a cardboard box. Perhaps most fortunate of all, they had called us at St Tiggywinkles Wildlife Hospital. At least we would not destroy him after seven days, as many organisations would.

The couple who had found him had had no means of getting him to Aylesbury and so I had called on one of our ever-willing team of volunteer 'ambulance' drivers to pick him up. I get many calls to go out to animals but would find it impossible if I had to attend every one, so volunteers such as Hywel and Jenni Johnes of St Albans are at the end of a phone any time, day or night. It was Hywel who went out on this cold, wet night to collect the 'mangey fox cub'. He did not look into the box but instead, with his heater full blast, drove as fast as he could to the Hospital.

The animal's condition was chronic, and so I gently laid him in a warm incubator. He could not stand up on his own. I offered a bowl of warmed Lectade to try to counter his general weakness and dehydration. He did not want to know and just lay there panting, his bottom jaw flapping drunkenly.

Les Stocker with a patient at St Tiggywinkles.

He had no teeth. How on earth could we get him to eat if he would not even drink? Perhaps he would take a small bowl of Luda dog food mixed with some water? This time he did not hesitate, and somehow he managed to scoop down mouthful after mouthful. He did appear to have one or two teeth at the back of his mouth, but every time we tried to look he growled the threatening sound of a dog which has not eaten for some time.

The vet who usually did our work was away, so the next morning I had to carry Baldrick, as the little dog became known, around to the veterinary surgery that had recently opened in our local parade of shops. Stella, the vet on duty, was as horrified as we were at his condition. She confirmed that he had part of his bottom jaw missing, which could only have been the result of a particularly hefty blow. He was, as we suspected, suffering from mange, but never had a dog been allowed to suffer with it for so long without treatment. To top these problems, Stella also detected a heart murmur and a fair amount of odoema (fluid) around the lungs. He was in a fine mess, but she thought he could be made comfortable and could live a happy life with us, providing he continued to eat. I picked him up when she had finished examining him. His little eyes watered as he cuddled up to me under my coat. We were not yet out of the woods.

It was going to take some weeks to cure the mange. Not for Baldrick the rapid ivermectin injections we now use to cure foxes. As these are fatal to some dogs, he would have to endure the weekly Alugan baths just like the first fox we successfully treated for mange (described in *Something in a Cardboard Box*). The only drawback to Alugan is that the animal has to drip dry. There could be no comfortable warm towel and cuddle. All we could do for Baldrick was put a heat lamp over his cage and talk to him as he lay there shivering next to an old cuddly teddy bear.

He soon warmed but seemed too frightened to sleep. Over the next three weeks, although everybody talked to him and cuddled him, he would rest only when his cage was completely covered with a blanket, as though he felt secure only in the darkness.

After four weeks of incarceration, his skin, although still devoid of hair, was smooth and healthy, like a billiard ball. All we had to do now was to get him to accept and come to terms with his new family life.

He could now, wearing his brand new warm raincoat, go out into the garden with our other two dogs, Cavalier spaniels Poppy and Sweep.

My wife Sue would fuss over him. He seemed to trust Sue from the very beginning, probably because she spoiled him outrageously – the proverbial Mother Hen clucking over and cuddling her foundling. Soon he took to sleeping next to Sue on the Chesterfield. He would never, unlike the other dogs, sit or lie on a lap, and he

A genuine fox cub casualty at St Tiggywinkles.

Baldrick – wearing his new raincoat – condescends to share a chair with Poppy and Sweep.

quivered and snapped in terror if he was woken suddenly. It took nearly six months for him to relax completely.

The vets could not guarantee that Baldrick would ever grow hair again but I think the good feeding and doggy-therapy paid off as he grew a good, if somewhat patchy, covering of fox-coloured hair. He had to have a quarter of a pill twice a day for his heart condition, but overall he made a remarkable transition from the skinny shivering waif of a 'fox' we originally took in to a small, if somewhat plump, confident little dog who dominated the household. The ravages of mange regularly turn wild animals into pathetic, skinny, shivering waifs, and often in the past sufferers were destroyed to put them 'out of their misery'. We now have utter confidence in being able to cure sarcoptic mange and have no hesitation in advising others to treat hedgehogs and foxes with Alugan acaricidal baths or ivermectin respectively.

In covering over 5,000 square kilometres of central England I have the sad privilege of rescuing many dozens of foxes, and the more I meet, the more I admire the resilience and expertise, rather than cunning, that has enabled them to survive the persecution heaped on them over the past two hundred years. Mrs Fox is the (not too original) name of one particular vixen I was honoured to meet, catch and treat. If ever a mother deserved the title 'Mother Courage', it was her.

In vain, I first tried to make her acquaintance on a blisteringly hot May afternoon in 1989. Worried workers at a local factory manufacturing concrete products called about a fox seriously debilitated with mange, who had, it seemed, touched every one of their hearts. I will not give any more details of the location as around here any mention of the word 'fox' brings every hunt supporter in the area running.

It appeared that I might need some help tracking Mrs Fox down so, leaving Sue in control of the Hospital, I took with me Michelle, our newly appointed veterinary nurse, together with Nikki, a stalwart member of our volunteer team.

When finally we had tracked our way through the jungle of concrete beams, cranes and giant cement mixers at the factory, the story we were told was so amazing and the loyalty of all those workers so heartening that we knew from the start that we could not rest until Mrs Fox had been found and made well once more.

Every one of those hulking great concrete workers was near to tears as they told how they had for months hand-fed her on sweets and other tit-bits. They told how she had found complete trust and sanctuary with them and just recently had made her nest in one of their storage sheds, producing six bonny, healthy cubs who now joined her in the freedom of the site. Now, though, each man was appalled how Mrs Fox was wasting away before their eyes. Her once glossy coat had almost all fallen out, replaced by the scabby soreness of mange, and just to make matters worse one of her back legs at times appeared to be too painful to put to the ground. She had taken to hobbling just a few yards and then collapsing with the exertion, but somehow she had found the strength to rear those six cubs, clearly determined to give them a good start to life before she succumbed.

My immediate quandary was which action to take. I could catch her and take her back to St Tiggywinkles for treatment, but how old were her cubs? Could they be left alone or would I have to catch all six of them as well? Could I just administer first aid? I could give a simple injection for the mange but that leg worried me, and with the baking weather she must surely be dehydrated. Mind you I had not seen her yet, even though every worker seemed to say, 'She was over there, only ten minutes ago.'

The three of us searched all that afternoon but found not a trace of the vixen although everywhere we caught glimpses of her cubs playing their own lightning version of hide-and-seek. I searched the shed where they were born and reared. It was now home to precarious mountains of old, derelict, greasy machinery that could snap a leg or crush a fox cub at the slightest disturbance. We searched the noisy factory itself, without success, and then we crawled around in the yard searching under every concrete girder. We managed to locate three of the gambolling cubs but could still find not a sign of their mother.

In the end we had to call it a day and return to the Hospital. I would get together a full rescue team and return later that evening when the factory was sleeping and deserted. For the time being I left Mrs Fox a pile of extremely smelly mice which had been defrosted some days previously. Their aroma would assail the nostrils of any fox round about and would I hoped tempt our vixen out into the open.

Eight of us returned in the evening. The quiet, deserted site seemed transformed: a local cuckoo revelled in the silence and sweet melodies of robins and thrushes mingled with the insistent 'tsees' of the finches. We arrived fully equipped and had even remembered our two short wave radios. This would surely mean success.

Splitting into groups we began by searching again the places where we had already been that afternoon. We drew a blank at the shed, the concrete girders appeared to be hiding nothing, and even the dark, empty expanses of the factory revealed only mice and a nest of starlings. We saw no sign of foxes, not even the three cubs who played with us earlier. We would have to extend our search area into the surrounding fields and undergrowth. We all rendezvoused at the south end of the site where I detailed Nigel Brock and Chris Kirk to take one of the radios and follow an obvious fox path through the boundary hedge into a neighbouring field.

They had not been gone for more than a couple of minutes before an urgent whispered crackle over the radio told me that a big fox had just run along their side of the hedge in our direction.

'Where is it now? Over,' I called back as I hurdled the concrete beams towards their position. 'It's coming through the end of the hedge towards you. It doesn't look injured. We are going to follow. Roger and out.' I must admit that when the radios come out we are all a little bit guilty of fighter-pilot mimicry. We just have to be careful that it does not impede our efficiency.

This time it may have done, for that was the last we heard from the other radio. It had probably been accidentally switched to another channel. Whether we liked it or not we had no option other than to maintain 'radio silence'.

I climbed to an excellent vantage point high

Meanwhile, back at the Hospital, Baldrick meets one of the hedgehogs.

above some derelict machinery and could soon make out a superb dog fox floating effortlessly through the shadows. This was obviously not our quarry but his proximity to the family site established him as the parent male. Dog foxes have been found quite capable of rearing cubs in the absence of the vixen, and this meant that all my decisions were that much easier to make. I could safely catch the vixen, take her back to the Hospital and treat her, returning her within a few days. I was very grateful not to have to catch all those cubs, who were already masters of the fox's artistry at disappearing and quite capable of gleaning a living from the offerings of the dog fox and staff at the concrete works.

We still had not seen any sign of the vixen. The dog fox knew where she was but was far too clever to aproach her. Instead, at a safe distance from us, he turned and howled what was possibly a greeting to his mate – or was it disapproval at our presence?

By now the dark clouds had started to bring the night rolling in. The songs of the cuckoo and the thrushes were being replaced by the screech of the local tawny owls and the high-pitched piping of the pipistrelle bats pouring from the roof of the factory. We continued the search with powerful torches but to no avail. I would have to muster my troops again the following night.

Having collected and reset the radio from the field search party, I set off across the site to retrieve my car and pack up all our equipment, nets and things ready for the next evening. I was

TIMELY TIPS

A dish of anglers' white maggots or meal-worms are safe bird-table fare in the summer months when dried food can be dangerous for nestlings.

Plant an extra few cabbages for the white butterflies.

Old rose and briar prunings and young this-tles will deter slugs and snails from raiding garden plants. There is no need to use chemical deterrents which are lethal to hedgehogs and garden birds.

Road accident victims that can be danger-ous include foxes, badgers and muntjac deer. Try to get any casualty to the side of the road, cover it to keep it warm and call for experienced assistance. Stay on the scene until help arrives but do not try to handle or console the animal. Take extreme care to keep clear of passing traffic.

Warmth and quiet are essential for any in-jured animal. Place the casualty in a card-board box with a covered hot-water bottle and then get it to the Hospital with the least possible delay.

If you spot an oiled bird, approach it from

the direction of the sea to prevent it trying to escape that way. Do not attempt to clean it. Cover it from the neck down to prevent it preening, and then call the Hospital for advice or the nearest trained bird-cleaning operative.

If a casualty has no outward signs of injury, it would greatly help our diagnosis if a note could be taken of any nearby crop-spraying or vermin-poisoning.

Why not knit a rope ladder to help spiders clamber out of your bath.

A biscuit tin fixed upside down at the top of a bird table pole will prevent cats and squirrels climbing to the platform.

If you should find a young deer lying in grass or cover *do not touch it*. The mother will be nearby and will react to your scent!

Never feed a young animal on pasteurised milk. If you cannot get the waif to the Hospital, feed it on Lactol available at most pet shops. However, baby birds should never be given milk in any form.

Check under potential bonfires before lighting. We treat many burnt hedgehogs every winter.

Sellotape laid sticky side up will deter cats from raiding nest boxes and approaching birds.

Plastic bags are slow to deteriorate and can cause suffocation. Tie them in a knot before disposing of them. Council rubbish sites are ideal foraging grounds for many species.

If you are having infested timbers treated make sure the contractors do not use Lindane or Dieldrin as these chemicals are lethal to bats. Synthetic pyrethroids are safe.

Never put an injured water bird or swan back onto water – keep it dry and warm.

Plant tomatoes close together to control couch grass. There is no need to use a herbicide.

Use only 'animal safe' water-based wood preservatives on fences and sheds.

Plant honeysuckle and hazel to help the decreasing dormouse population.

Make sure all drains, especially small ones, are covered at all times.

Use cardboard pet-carrying boxes, available from vets or pet shops, to send hedgehog casualties by Red Star or Interlink.

Don't try to get an injured bird to drink – just keep it warm and dark until expert help can be obtained.

Molehills make excellent potting compost.

Keep netting 23 centimetres above the ground.

driving back in the now total darkness when suddenly I picked up two bright lights in my headlights. They were fox eyes peering unblinking back at me from under a pile of girders. Could they be our vixen, or just another cub? Quickly I switched the radio on, hoping that Andy Walton, another of our rescue team, also had his receiver switched on. He had, and following my directions deployed the rest of the team, with their powerful torches, to cover my headlight beam still holding the fox in its brightness.

Andy was the first to approach the fox, and sensing his presence it limped off into the darkness. With his torch he quickly picked out the scarred, painfully thin animal trying to hide in the shadows. This was surely our vixen and judging by her condition she would be comparatively easy to catch.

Wrong! For a fox who relished the company of humans she did all in her power to avoid any contact whatsoever with these ones and for over fifteen minutes led us in and out of all sizes of those infernal concrete girders. This was a very sick fox but she still had complete mastery of the situation, and finally slid under a veritable mountain of giant iron panels that even an elephant could not move. By hanging upside-down between girders, and with my head resting on the grass, I could see into her new lair. It was impregnable and she knew it, as she grinned at me from the limit of my torch's beam. After a half-hour's fruitless banging we called the search off for the night, deciding to leave a cage trap that would catch her without harming her.

We were all disappointed at having been 'so near and yet so far', but the whole evening had had its magic, because of the birds and because of that majestic dog fox. Everyone volunteered to come the following evening to try again. This is surely the essence of wildlife rescue and care: try, try and try again, and never ever give up.

Early the following morning I returned, on my own, to check the trap and if necessary to release any other animal that might have blundered into it.

The trap had not been visited and for once the workers thereabouts had seen no sign of the vixen. I was about to change the bait in the trap when another man came panting across the tarmac trying to shout above the noise of the heavy machinery that was back at work again. 'She's down the other end. Been there since early morning. She took part of my lunch box!'

Here we go again.

'Jump in,' I insisted – almost snapped – while slamming my car boot. The sooner I got to the other end of the site the more chance I had of at least seeing this elusive fox.

It was about 400 metres along dirt track to the rubbish dump where she had been seen. I left a great dust cloud in my wake as I sped across the site but I was still too late. She had disappeared again.

There was a chance that she might have scrambled down a very steep bank to drink from a nearby stream but a young squirrel frolicking

Poppy always showed an interest in the patients.

at the water's edge told me that there was not a fox around. She could not have gone far – the day was just as hot as the previous one, and she would not want to travel in the dust. She would probably be lying low, looking at us, perhaps realising that we were trying to catch her.

Then all of a sudden a giant tipper lorry skidded to a halt in the dust, right up against the back of my hastily parked car.

Thinking I was blocking his way I immediately made to move my car.

''Ave you got 'er?' bellowed the driver from way up in his cab.

Assuming he meant the vixen I replied, 'I haven't even seen her.'

I will ignore his expletives but it will suffice to say that this driver, only a visitor to the site, had nearly run over our vixen. She had sat calmly on the track and let him walk right up to her. Having no sandwiches or titbits to offer, he had promptly reversed off the site in order to phone for help. Before he could return, we had arrived and she had departed. The driver was just as flummoxed as we were with her disappearance. By now, if I had not seen her the night before I would have sworn I was the victim of a complicated hoax.

''Ave you got 'er yet?'

Another voice approached, which no doubt belonged to someone who regularly fed our errant vixen. Yes, but this man went one better. He had known her since she was a cub.

Mrs Fox on the road to recovery.

'Born over there under those girders, two years ago,' he pointed to an overgrown heap right next to the boundary hedge. 'At this time of day she'll be lying just over there under those girders.'

And there she was at last. Tucked away in the shade, a coiled bundle of tattiness lying helpless under a girder. However, even now she was not so helpless, and seeing us approaching she limped off as fast as she could. But this time there were no giant iron panels to hide under and in a trice we had her in the net and then safely ensconced in a carrying basket.

Now we could see in all its horrible detail the sarcoptic mange that had so dragged her down and the injured leg swollen to three times its normal size. All her fight had gone now and she sank resigned and worn out to the bottom of the basket, completely exhausted by that short final flurry before we caught her.

Back at the Hospital her condition demanded an intravenous drip of fluid therapy just to keep her alive. I started a course of antibiotics, in case the swollen leg was infected. An injection of ivermectin sounded the first death knell for the mange mites that had tormented her for so long. Then after all the manhandling I laid her in a warm recovery cage expecting the worst.

For two days she could neither eat nor drink and seemed slowly but surely to be sinking into oblivion. Michelle and I continued nursing her until her third day of antibiotic injections, when I told Michelle to get a 19g needle and penetrate that swollen leg. As she plunged the needle in, thick pus oozed out. The leg was indeed grossly infected. There was now no alternative: the leg would have to be opened up and the infected tissues cleaned away. Also, there was a fear that Mrs Fox had a dislocated hip, and this could also be put back in place while she was under anaesthetic.

Monitoring the depth of anaesthesia, Michelle checked the fox's gums for pinkness, a sign of good circulation. Her gasp of horror made everybody jump, but there it was — a distinct yellowing of the gums. This is a possible sign of leptospirosis, the highly contagious disease spread by rats which can cause the potentially fatal Weil's disease in humans.

Obviously we were all worried, and even more so when we found out that the normal veterinary procedure of sending away samples and waiting for a result takes fourteen days, by which time any infection could really take a hold. However, being virtually next door to Stoke Mandeville Hospital, and knowing some of the staff, I thought we might try the superb micro-biology department there to see if they could possibly give us some immediate answers.

John, one of the micro-biologists, agreed to test samples of the fox's blood and urine, and also offered to help if any of us at St Tiggywinkles had been unnecessarily exposed to risk. For the time being I kept Mrs Fox in isolation and made sure everybody washed their hands in strong disinfectant. It's never advisable to 'scrub' hands in this situation just in case the brush opens up an old scratch or lesion allowing

infection to gain a foothold. Of course if the tests were positive then we would have to let common sense prevail and put the fox to sleep. I know this seems contrary to all my beliefs that an animal should be kept alive at all costs, but the professional reputation we have fought for and built up over the years would be destroyed if I willingly exposed any one of us to potentially lethal organisms. But we just had to wait for the results of the tests, and this seemed to take hours. None of us went near Mrs Fox but we all marched up and down and chain-smoked just like expectant fathers.

Eventually, after three hours that seemed more like thirty, John phoned to say the samples were clear of leptospirosis. The relief was immediate, and we all with one accord dived straight back to nursing poor old Mrs Fox.

However, Mrs Fox herself did not feel at all downhearted and the following day, with her leg obviously feeling much better, she started to move around her box and tear up her bedding in a welter of water, dog food and other indescribables, in good fox fashion. Then she began tentatively to feel the floor with her bad leg, and before long she succeeded in walking on it. On the third day after her operation she actually stood on her hind legs to try to tear the wire roof off her box — all great fox behaviour. I felt that now we could reasonably take her back to her concrete factory, where I knew that all the staff would keep a very close eye on her.

When we took her out she still looked

painfully thin and she still limped on that damaged leg but she would be better off with her family and all those people whom she knew and trusted. I let her see me put down a large mound of frozen mice, just in case she was hungry, and then Sue opened her carrying cage. For a while she hesitated, then seeming to sense her own territory she slowly slid, once more, back among the girders to join her family.

For Baldrick, however, there was no way back to a family, and anyway judging by his ill-treated condition I doubt if he would want to return to a life of misery. There are so many things we shall never know about him. Even his breed was in doubt for a long while, but as he grew more hair we finally settled for a Pomeranian. We shall never know his proper name, even though I have assailed him with all manner of 'Pepes' and 'Fidos', and even the occasional 'Rover'. Not one of them has provoked even a modicum of recognition – mind you, he is a master at playing deaf when it suits him, although I know he can hear the biscuit tin opening no matter how quiet I am.

He has now recovered a funny little staccato bark and soon lets us know if he wants anything, especially his routine tit-bit while I am eating

my Weetabix in the mornings. He settled early on with Poppy and Sweep but never appeared to grow very close to them, even during the four days when they were all confined to our bedroom while we were making the video to back our appeal for funds for our new Hospital.

Then one morning Poppy had some form of heart attack. We took her to the vet, who carried out some tests to establish what had happened. While we waited for the result, Poppy lay stretched out on an armchair, breathing quite noisily. Suddenly Baldrick leapt up beside her and started licking her face as though trying to comfort her.

I do not know how he sensed that she was so very ill, but ten minutes later, while Sue was holding her paw, Poppy's heart stopped for the last time.

Why do we always do it? Bring a pet into the family and suffer terribly when inevitably it dies? Baldrick, we think, is quite elderly and we know it could happen at any time. But for the moment he is happy, warm and secure.

LEFT *For a while she hesitated, and then she slid away under the girders.*

2 Pets and Parliaments

Since moving to Aylesbury from Raynes Park in 1970, we have enjoyed sharing our home with pet dogs. Until Baldrick took over our lives our dogs were always Cavalier King Charles spaniels. Poppy had added to the household by having five pups, of which we still had one, Sweep. We have taken in various other pets which were lost or abandoned, but when wild animals dictate your life it is unfair to ask a pampered pet bird or temperamental reptile to become just one of the crowd. The dogs are different – they can live in the house as part of the family – but pet birds or reptiles need their own quarters and far more time and attention than we can adequately give them. Luckily many of our volunteer team are more than willing to provide a home for the occasional vagrant.

We had almost no garden at our first house in Aylesbury but when we moved, in 1978, to Pemberton Close, we had a fairly large garden with a sizable grassed area ideal for tortoises. I say that because no sooner had we moved in than Sue spotted two pathetic-looking tortoises in a pet shop in deepest Surrey. I had only one or two bird casualties at the time so there was plenty of space for them to set up home on the back lawn. However, as anyone who has ever lived with a tortoise knows, for vertebrates very low down the evolutionary scale, without a modicum of intelligence, tortoises seem to be reincarnations of Houdini – ours were forever escaping in spite of the metre-high chain link fence which separated them from the next door garden. Costas and Heather, his wife, were always having to retrieve itinerant tortoises blundering their way through their grow-bags.

Then, one day, Moogli, the most adventurous of the tortoises, managed even to escape Costas's garden – he disappeared without trace. We asked all the other neighbours in Pemberton Close but to no avail ... until a mother at the bottom of the road seemed to remember her somewhat unruly children playing with a tortoise. A cuffed ear from his mother brought the response from the largest boy, about nine years old, that he had sold a tortoise to another boy the other side of the railway tracks on the Stoke Mandeville housing estate. Another cuffed ear sent the children scurrying under the railway to repossess the tortoise. It was Moogli, who was soon returned to his lawn. I scoured the chain link fence with a fine-toothed comb and, finding no gaps, made sure that the bottom was securely anchored to the ground so that Moogli could not squeeze underneath.

Contrary to popular opinion, tortoises are difficult animals to keep healthy, requiring constantly warm temperatures, especially during the summer months, to encourage them to eat enough to put on fat reserves to survive hibernation in the winter. Should the temperatures remain low, as has been the case in recent summers, then the tortoises become lethargic and often will not feed. According to the textbooks, tortoises should eat vast quantities of fresh green vegetable matter, liberally varied with fruit, tomatoes and essential vitamins, with occasional meat products to provide extra protein. The trouble with our tortoises was that they did not seem to have read the textbooks and thrived on a diet of grass and lettuce and any herbaceous border plants that I was fool enough to sow. As a meat substitute Honshu, the other tortoise, took great delight in biting toes, especially Sue's when she wore her open-toed sandals.

Yet in spite of this totally 'inadequate' diet our two tortoises thrived for many years and are still doing so. Inevitably other tortoises with wanderlust arrived from various obscure locations around Aylesbury, including the High Street, the local tip and the Chiltern Forest, a few kilometres down the road. Nobody ever came forward to claim their truants. But this casual state of affairs was before the current legislation which restricts importing and dealing in tortoises. Now tortoises are worth a lot of money so either people are not buying them or they are making very sure that they do not escape. However, the legislation put no restriction on the import of box turtles. These are sold as tortoises but are in fact carnivorous turtles that would soon perish on a tortoise's diet. When one unfortunate box turtle turned up at the Hospital, I made sure it went to an animal expert used to caring for exotic creatures.

The only recent tortoise to arrive, whose owners cared enough to come and collect him, was a small male of boundless energy. There are ways of sexing tortoises – the male has a concave carapace – but this little tortoise left us in no doubt about his gender as he systematically turned his attentions to each of our flower-eating females. This was not the love-making of a sedate animal, but a frantic, open-mouthed gasping session pre-empted by an incessant barrage of head butts to the flank of the victim.

Bonkers, as he became known, was only with us for about a week. I am sure there was a sigh of relief from the other seven when his owners took him away.

My seven female tortoises could devote most of their attention to munching their way through my borders. They were a regular part of the garden scene, mixing unconcernedly with any free-living resident casualties. This had its advantages for the other inmates. Tortoises are masters (or mistresses) at absorbing and retaining heat from the sun. This means that on fine days tortoises are warm to the touch. Jonathan the resident black-headed gull (what else?) soon cottoned on to this and every afternoon would hitch a free ride on a warm back. Soon other birds, especially collared doves, started to emulate Jonathan's feet-warming exercises. The garden would look like a surrealist circus, as various birds, some with splints on their wings, were carried jerkily around by unconcerned tortoises.

In 1988 as we became busier and busier it became harder to maintain the individual and specialised attention demanded by the tortoises. Hedgehogs build their own nests in which to hibernate and do not need protection from frosts and cold weather. With tortoises, on the other hand, you have to provide a hay-filled box, starve them for a couple of days and then secrete their hibernaculum in some frost-free part of a building. I think that I finally decided to part with them when one winter they just would not hibernate and I would regularly find them wandering around the floor of the garage. I had no alternative but to transfer them to one of our few heated cages to keep them awake and feed them for the winter.

Wincey Willis has always been very interested in tortoises and has, at her cottage, a specially designed building with bespoke heating arrangements tailored to the needs of her own tortoises. Wincey kindly agreed to take on our tortoises and the precious heated cage could be released for use on genuine casualties.

I described in *Something in a Cardboard Box* how we had to find new homes for a vagrant python, terrapins and a majestic Bosc monitor. I would have loved to keep them but could not subject them to life in a busy hospital. As well as these celebrities there were oddities such as the tiny green tree frog which turned up at a local fruiterers, hiding in a consignment of oranges, soon followed by the Spanish lizard which popped its head out of some imported melons. Exotic birds often escape and, being unable to cope with life in wild Britain, end up on our doorstep. Homes have readily been found for various budgies and Zebra finches, and for some noisy cockatiels, one of which shook me at first by giving a perfect rendition of the first few bars of 'Pop goes the weasel'. When I first heard the whistle, wafting in through the dining room window, I thought there was a person whistling in the garden.

Jonathan would hitch a ride on a warm back.

Larger birds are occasionally brought in. A very handsome ring-necked parakeet arrived and, although there is now a breeding population of these birds in Britain, it is illegal to release them. Even if this were not the case, the British climate is not really suitable for exotic birds and to release non-indigenous species could anyway, in my mind, constitute a crime against the ecological balance of nature. Jenni and Hywel agreed to adopt him and now Busby, as he was named, rules the roost and has turned their way of life upside down.

'Colonel', another casualty brought to the Hospital, was we decided a blue-headed Amazon parrot of great age. His beak was pitted and broken, most of his toes were non-existent and his whole general demeanour was one of refined senility. Mind you, that broken and pitted beak could still make mincemeat of any unwary finger, as I found out to my cost. In spite of his tortuous attacks on my finger and because of his old age, we decided to let him live out his last days with us, spoilt and mollycoddled to the end.

In the case of small birds we do ask people to put any casualties in cardboard boxes and bring them to the Hospital. However there are often occasions when we have to mobilise a rescue even for the much-maligned 'townie' pigeons which give many people much pleasure and entertainment as they scavenge in and out of the feet of passers-by. In Aylesbury there always

Colonel, the stray parrot.

seems to be a shop or store closed down and behind these dirty shop fronts pigeons are occasionally seen scavenging in the dust among the empty counters and piles of unopened mail. Often they are fed through the letter boxes but there is no way of getting water to them so gradually they go downhill. Invariably there is no obvious way they could have got into the empty buildings, and being 'bird-brains' they can never find their way out.

We regularly receive calls about such birds and rather than resort to smashing the windows we have to go through the rigmarole of contacting the estate agents, who are always in London, then tracking down a key to the premises, and finally catching the often uncooperative pigeon for a few days recuperation at the Hospital. If we kept them any longer they would never leave – even after release they would unerringly home in on the free food put out for our long-stay pigeons.

We have four resident woodpigeons who cannot fly, for one reason or another. These live out their lives in the freedom of the garden and have set up home under the office where their billing and cooing and constant bickering keep us all amused. The only trouble is that their bowls of corn do attract local pigeons, especially the large flock of racers from about three doors away. Every morning the owner lets this flock out for exercise, which to them means taking the short hop into our garden with its endless supply of corn. I bet they are all too fat to win any races.

The small relative of the pigeon, the collared dove, only ever seems to visit our garden in pairs. They are small, light brown birds, with the daintiest faces and eyes. They were non-existent in Britain before 1952 but have gradually, for some unknown reason, colonised the whole of the country. They are quite a common bird now, which in some ways is a pity, as they are no longer protected and have become cannon fodder for the gun-toting fraternity.

As well as being shot, collared doves are among the hundred million annual victims of our oversized cat population. But they are also one of the few casualties we take in with a purely natural affliction – in this case trichomoniasis, caused by flagellate protozoans (small single-celled animals) taken in while feeding from the throat of a parent. In addition they have peculiar accidents: they fall down chimneys, they fly into windows, and one bird we took in had somehow managed to force its top beak clean through its bottom beak, with the result that it could not feed. It is nigh on impossible to catch any casualty which still has the power of flight. It's only when the bird has become so weak from starvation that it can be caught and treated. This is why I tell anybody taking in injured birds that if a wild bird can be caught it is more than likely dying, so that if it does die it is probably no reflection on the rescuer's treatment. And of course if it survives, it is a bonus.

I managed to untangle the collared dove's beak and after a few weeks' good feeding at the Hospital it was fit for release.

The collared dove with its top beak through its bottom beak – an easily remedied complaint.

When fledgling collared doves are brought to us they cannot readily be carried in their nests, unlike young thrushes and blackbirds, as the extremely fragile twig platforms disintegrate at the slightest opportunity. But we did receive one couple of young collared doves still in the nest – in fact, still in the tree, which was also brought in! Apparently nobody saw the two little birds hanging on for grim death as their tree was being cut away from under them. Only when it was nearly down did somebody spot them and bring the whole thing in to us.

Actually this ridiculous situation had been

predicted by the renowned cartoonist Bill Tidy who Sue and I met at the TV-am studios as we all waited to go on the early morning show. Bill, unable to sit doing nothing, quickly rushed off a cartoon of a casualty, in this case a squirrel, being brought into the Hospital complete with its own tree. The strangest things do actually happen!

On one occasion we were called out to a large exhaust and tyre depot in Aylesbury town centre, which had a voluminous fitting area about 20 metres long and 6 metres high. The front of the building consists of 3-metre-high sliding doors topped by large glass unopening windows of a similar height. It was behind these enormous windows that a pair of collared doves were trapped, quite unable to work out that they could at any time fly down and through the open doors.

I went out on this 'rescue' because, once again, there was no food or water accessible to the two birds. My first attempts to catch them in the vast cavern of the roof space were mocked by their dexterity in flying just over my net as it swayed crazily at the end of a waving 3-metre pole.

All along this fitting bay were hydraulic ramps for lifting cars up above head height.

IT WOULD HAVE BEEN PERFECTLY OK IF YOU'D JUST BROUGHT THE SQUIRREL "

With the assistance of one of the fitters, I stood on a ramp as he raised it about 2 metres above the ground. Fine, I could now reach the ceiling, but the birds could fly out sideways, which they did every time I waved my net at them. The next ploy was first to move them down to one end, and then to drop my ramp and jump on one nearer them which could be raised as I leapt on.

Back and forth and up and down we went for ages until all four ramps were in use, but I still had not caught even one of the doves. But then one flew behind a shield on the window and with some difficulty, and balancing one-legged on top of one of the ramp supports, I managed to net him. In panic the other dove flew straight down to the fitter who grabbed it with very little ceremony. Then it was back to the Hospital for twenty-four hours' recuperation for the doves – and for me, completely out of breath from all that ramp jumping.

Mind you, I still had to call in on the canal where a duck was reputedly in trouble. Aylesbury is world famous as the home of the Aylesbury Duck but, although I hate to disappoint you, there is not an Aylesbury Duck anywhere near Aylesbury. In fact the renowned duck industry died out early this century. The trouble is that well-meaning people keep introducing white ducks to any spare stretch of water in the Town. There are two problems with this: firstly, the white ducks with orange beaks which they introduce are not true Aylesburys, which have a flesh-coloured beak; and, secondly, these cross-bred ducks, just like the Aylesburys, are often unable to fly and are consequently regularly being caught in all manner of ways and are 'sitting ducks' to children with air-guns and cross-bows.

I once wrote a potted history of the Aylesbury Duck and, in my research, found out that the original duck industry flourished in people's gardens. The Aylesburys were never allowed onto open water and were always protected from predators and people. In fact I learnt a lot from the experiences of those old Aylesburians

The only Aylesbury Duck in Aylesbury these days is on a pub sign.

The Aylesbury Duck industry used to flourish in the town.

about keeping my wild casualty ducks. Until I did that work I had found it extremely difficult to keep orphaned ducklings alive. The first revelation was that ducklings are not waterproof and if allowed to bathe for any length of time will quite readily chill and die. The old Aylesbury people did not allow their ducks onto water until they were fifteen weeks old and fully grown.

The other tip which I picked up and which has proved invaluable, both to ducklings and other precocious young birds, is to provide a surrogate mother in the form of a feather duster which they will confidently snuggle under. So far this year we have successfully reared over twenty duck orphans with these methods and not one of them was allowed to swim until it was fully grown.

The duck in trouble on the canal was a white one. As these white ducks are classed as being owned and the responsibility of whoever released them in the first place we aren't, in fact, allowed to treat them. In this case I had a good idea who the owner was and called on him in the next street to the canal, and informed him of the injured duck and of his responsibilities towards it.

I was quite relieved at not having to catch that particular casualty – even if a duck cannot fly it is the most elusive of quarries, running across the water at a furious rate and then, just when you think you have it in your net, diving and surfacing many metres away. And when ducks can fly as well – not with the slow run-up of the swan or goose but with an explosive take-off straight up – you have very little chance of catching them. This is so frustrating because it means that there are ducks flying around with broken legs, or fishing line dangling from their beaks or, most horrifying of all, with a deadly plastic necklace from the top of a four-pack of beer. I do wish that when people throw away these plastic rings they would cut through each loop so that it will not eventually ensnare a bird or a small mammal. Perhaps some form of legislation on the manufacturers would force them to invent an alternative.

I am not one who willy-nilly campaigns for more cumbersome legislation but in some cases I feel that there really is no alternative. Take, for example, the hedgehog: a small, inoffensive, often helpful and extremely popular British mammal. At present there is very little, if any, protection for hedgehogs, yet one simple piece of protective legislation would harm nobody and prove to be very popular with the British voters.

The trouble with a great deal of wildlife legislation and its supporters is that it hides behind numbers. 'If an animal is reasonably prolific then why should it be protected?' they ask.

'Poppycock!' I say. For instance, most wild birds enjoy full protection, and so do their nest sites, and yet there is no shortage of many bird species. In fact their numbers are often counted in millions. So why not go for similar protection for hedgehogs, both under the Protection of Animals Act 1911 and the Wildlife and Countryside Act 1981? The quinquennial review of the 1981 Act was coming up in 1988, so would it not be just a stroke of a pen for the Minister to give hedgehogs the protection they warrant?

Over the last couple of years we had, with the wonderful efforts of all the members of the Trust, amassed a petition asking for the protection of hedgehogs. There were over 36,000 signatures, producing a mountain of petition sheets which with the advice of two great anonymous supporters (shall we just say Jane and Martin) we managed to get worded correctly and bound into seven handsome volumes for presentation to the Earl of Caithness, Minister of State for the Environment.

After the wonderful screed of wording that has to be at the front of such a petition, and the signature of Robert B. Jones, Member of Parliament for West Hertfordshire, who was submitting the petition, came the signatures of Sue and me, overshadowed by those of Sir David Attenborough, Dennis Furnell, Bill Oddie, Wincey Willis and many other 'big guns' in an effort to make the petition successful.

At the time I had, ready for release, over fifty fully fit-to-go hedgehogs. As these would be

The Hospital contingent set off at 7.30 a.m.

released into gardens in twos or threes I told the fosterers that they would have to collect their charges from Parliament Square as the petition was handed over. We wanted to look our best for the media who were bound to be present, and so Peter Kemp of Shaw's Pet Products supplied us with three dozen of their very smart pet-carrying boxes. At 7.30 a.m., 29 people, 36 pet-carrying boxes, 7 volumes of petition and, of course, 54 hedgehogs set off in a hired coach. Our rendezvous at Westminster with Robert Jones and the media was to be 9.30 a.m., giving us two hours to get there, which seemed ample time.

I should have known better. As we approached Chelsea the already heavy traffic ground to a standstill – it turned out we had chosen the day of the Chelsea Flower Show to attempt our hedgehog invasion of central London.

An eternity later we passed Lambeth Bridge. Our goal was in sight as we could see Parliament Square in the distance. But our driver had an ace up her sleeve. 'I can't stop on the square. I'll have to drop you here.' About 300 metres short of our rendezvous.

There was nothing for it but for Sue to run on ahead to let our reception committee know we had arrived. Sue probably had not had to run anywhere for the past ten years but she showed a resolve and a clean pair of heels in her anxiety to get there. On the last leg she came upon the

The very helpful policewoman in Parliament Square.

incessant stream of traffic which forever circles Parliament Square, but luckily a compassionate policewoman saw her plight and did a 'Moses and the Red Sea' with the traffic to let her across the road.

Fortunately everybody had been prepared to wait for the main party with the petition, and for all those hedgehogs. It even turned out that the very helpful policewoman had phoned us several times over the previous three years as she was herself looking after a disabled hedgehog.

Robert took the petition, the television crews and newspapermen took their pictures, the foster team carried off their hedgehogs and we all made our way back to the coach – which had disappeared. Our driver had thought it better to park about a kilometre away, but regretfully had not thought to inform us.

Eventually, we found the coach and drove home exhausted (incidentally, via some new traffic jams in the Hammersmith and Shepherds Bush Roads).

Robert Jones had been very understanding about our late arrival and I must say that to our surprise we have always found Parliamentarians to be kind and most tolerant even if somewhat slow to come up with the much-needed wildlife legislation. However, we are told that in 1992 we shall all become 'Europeans' and our wildlife legislation may be made more effective by the European Parliament. Our local Member of the European Parliament, James Elles, has visited the Hospital on a number of occasions and shows a great interest in the work we are doing. His first visit sticks in my mind. As he was shown around the intensive care unit, which as usual had received its daily scrub-out, he stopped at one cage and asked Sue, 'How often do you clean out these cages?'

Sue, of course, replied proudly, 'Every day.'

'I don't think that can be quite right,' said Mr Elles, flooring Sue with this attack.

'Oh, I do assure you we do,' spluttered Sue, very taken aback.

'Then,' said Mr Elles, 'how come this newspaper hasn't been changed since 1939?'

I looked into the cage he indicated and the headline shouted out at me: 'Graf Spee Scuttled Last Night'. It was true, one of our volunteer team had lined the cage with a copy of the *Daily Telegraph* dated Monday 18th December 1939. Of course we all laughed as I retrieved the newspaper for posterity and attempted to wipe off the splodgy mess with which the hedgehogs had already managed to desecrate the front page.

We do not know where the newspaper came from and in spite of a detailed search of our newspaper stocks we have failed to find any other historical documents.

3 All Our Wild Animals Bite

Our Member of the European Parliament has, so far, come through his involvement with the St Tiggywinkles Wildlife Hospital unscathed. Not so Robert Jones, who was one of the first of a whole list of VIPs who have been savaged, if you can use that strong a word, by our hedgehogs. Robert is the champion of hedgehogs in Parliament, despite being bitten by one during a photocall for one of the national newspapers. Colin Baker has now been bitten more times by our hedgehogs than he has been attacked by Daleks as Doctor Who. Michaela Strachan of TV-am's 'Wide-awake Club' still remarks upon her encounter with one of our sabre-toothed hedgehogs, while Howard Stapleforth, presenting John Craven's Newsround, actually dropped his hedgehog on film.

Fortunately a hedgehog's bite is not too serious. Being insectivores they have quite small teeth and cannot exert a lot of pressure with their jaws – that is, unless they practise. I happily used to let Patches, the hedgehog whose

Robert Jones was the first VIP to be savaged by one of the hedgehogs.

skin I had stitched back together after a road accident, latch onto my finger to give demonstrations of the harmless hedgehog bite. That was until one day all his practice finally made perfect and the demonstration had me shouting in pain as his new prowess threatened to crush my finger. Patches travels with me quite often and has become something of a television celebrity. However he still occasionally blots his copybook and recently nearly disabled a technician on another television programme aptly called 'Motormouth'. Mind you, I had warned the technician that Patches might bite. Recently on a breakfast programme the presenter, Mike Morris, was lining himself up to get bitten, but he took my warning just in time and withdrew his finger like lightning, to the amusement of the watching public.

Most hedgehogs will never attempt to bite; it's only the exceptions like master-fang Patches who will launch into unprovoked attacks. But even then, although the bite may be painful, the hedgehog does not really cause any damage.

Not so the squirrel, which is probably the most difficult mammal to handle and possesses

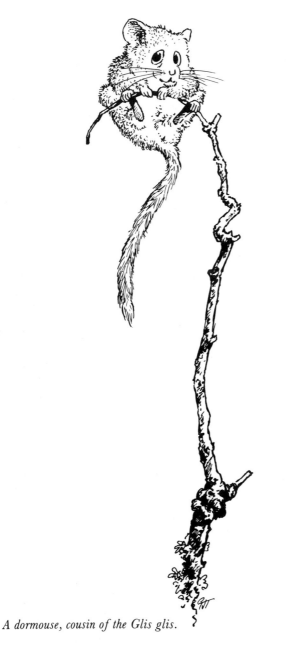

A dormouse, cousin of the Glis glis.

a super-bite – its incisors only stop penetrating when they hit bone. I regularly wear my thick welder's gloves when handling squirrels. In fact gloves are quite a hindrance in handling mammals and I would not contemplate wearing them for any other species, except perhaps the squirrel look-alike, Glis glis. I very seldom get bitten (touch wood), and even when I do it always seems to be by tame animals. It's invariably my own fault in being a little complacent with tame animals whereas I never give a wild animal the opportunity to bite.

Chestnut, our resident disabled squirrel, is usually very docile and friendly, liking nothing better than to have his chest or ears tickled by all and sundry. There is only one thing that Chestnut will not tolerate and that is being picked up against his will. Pick him up and he will bite, and the worst of it is that he attacks in a lightning dash of awe-inspiring ferocity. I have been bitten three times in the five years that he has lived with us, twice in the cause of duty – rescuing volunteers who had attempted to pick him up – and the third time quite recently when the neighbourhood ginger cat sent him crazy with fear as it stalked across the wire-mesh roof of his pen. The cat had managed to break into the aviary next door, sending the birds into demented panic as well, as it set about a ruthless massacre. Five birds were ripped to death before I heard the pandemonium and ran in to save the rest. Having to

RIGHT *Chestnut, the Hospital's resident squirrel.*

Barney Rubble the stone curlew before his wing operation.

pass through Chestnut's pen to get into the aviary I did not take much notice of his jumping onto my shoulder as he usually did. However, his chattering teeth, close to my ear, told me I was in for trouble unless I got him off at once. He was biting everything in sight, including my fingers as I gently, but quickly, lifted him onto his perch.

Immediately I dived, out of harm's way, into the bird aviary with its carnage. There were dead birds and feathers everywhere and lying in the corner was the still, still form of Barney Rubble, the exceedingly rare stone curlew whose recovery from the collision that had destroyed his right wing had been well underway. After the wing had been amputated I had hoped to get another captive stone curlew from one of the zoos and attempt to get them to breed in the confines of the aviary. Then, any offspring could be released into the wild in Suffolk, where Barney had been found, to swell the meagre British breeding population of an estimated two hundred birds. The ginger cat had just put paid to all those plans.

The cat, whose owner we could not trace, had been pestering our birds for a long time. I had tried all manner of tactics to discourage his visits, even resorting to the recommended hosing with water technique. Sweep regularly led the charge to get rid of the cat, careering mindlessly round the garden barking threateningly – all to no avail. The cat just looked at both of us and grinned.

Then my chance arose. The ginger cat was sitting defiantly in the middle of the road as I drove in. As I performed the perfect emergency stop I wondered how many times he had escaped being run over. He grinned at me once more.

I had read in *Cage and Aviary Birds* newspaper of a new anti-cat defence used harmlessly but successfully by many aviculturists. It was a very low voltage electric fence that did no harm to the cats but merely discouraged them from crossing it. This seemed the answer but, in spite of numerous phone calls and duplicate written orders, the electric fence never arrived.

I plotted and plotted. My ultimate brainwave was to live-trap him and find him a home as far away from Aylesbury as possible. We occasionally have to live-trap foxes and other animals that are injured but still able to elude capture, in order that we can treat them. One night I baited a fox trap with a particularly smelly herring. Halfway through the evening I heard it slam shut. Expecting to meet a tiger I approached the trap cautiously, only to be met by a happy hedgehog digging in to a meal of herring.

I removed him and put him in another part of the garden where he could not interfere with the trap. I reset the trap with the remains of the smelly herring and sat at the dining room window and waited. I could not see anything but, after a short while, heard the 'clang' as the trap shut.

I had caught Ginger, and now my mind ran riot with all sorts of plans to get rid of him. I walked up to the trap, and this time I was grinning. But he looked up at me and miaowed pathetically. I opened the trap and let him go.

He still pesters me. Four times today Sweep has become frantic in his efforts to get at him. Mind you, the only time Sweep ever managed to reach a cat he stopped short, perplexed about what to do next. The cat swiped him on the nose and that settled it – he ran. Ginger has seen it all before and just sits on Nigel's garage, next door, and grins at Sweep's ineffectiveness. He still causes panic in the aviary and often upsets Chestnut, whom I am careful to console from outside his pen.

On that occasion when Chestnut did manage to bite me, I had a job to stop my fingers bleeding. But I just had to press on and hope for the best, as I had arranged that morning to collect Becky, a tame badger, from Sally Reynold's farm on the other side of Tring, and take her to the vet's for treatment to wounds that had appeared on her rump.

I had known Becky since she was a cub, when I had taken her for fostering from another animal welfare group. From the moment I first picked her up I could see how tame she was and, with sinking heart, realised that she could never be released – or so I thought. She was glorious, a real live black-and-white teddy bear who would play from dawn to dusk, never seeming to tire and with never an aggressive gesture. She obviously needed a good, caring home where she would have plenty of room to play and dig and do all the things a badger loves to do. Sally, on her large, safe farm, had adopted some of our other large animals. Bambi and Fate, the two fallow deer, with various ducks and geese, had the freedom of many hundreds of acres.

I rang Sally and explained Becky's predicament. I need not have worried, for Sally jumped at the chance of taking on this roly-poly bundle of badger.

Sally made Becky a home in one of the wonderful old barns that are such a feature of her farm. I could envisage Sally spending most of her time with Becky and I was not far wrong. Each time I visited I would find the pair of them in the barn, with Becky curled up on Sally's lap.

Then one night Becky managed to break out of the barn while Sally was asleep in bed. By the morning, she had returned, mucky and exhausted, but pronking around, obviously very pleased with her little excursion, as Sally went in.

Becky before her first 'escapade'.

These little forays became a nightly occurrence, with Becky back every morning waiting for her breakfast. But it had to happen and it did: one morning the barn was empty. Sally searched every corner of the farm, calling Becky, waving her favourite Milky Way bars in the air, but there was no sign of her. For three days and nights Sally searched in vain and then, as suddenly as she had disappeared, there she was, all snuggled up in her favourite paper sack. Sally, relieved, scolded her through the bag but there was no response from Becky. Sally tilted the bag as she had done dozens of times before but this time Becky let out a low, rumbling growl. A wave of a Milky Way soon brought a more amiable response, followed by a twitching nose and then a very muddy badger. Last of all to leave the sack in pursuit of the Milky Way was a horribly bloody rump. Becky had been fighting with another badger and had come home to lick her wounds.

She would not let Sally anywhere near the sore places, so this is where I came in. The strategy was to take her to the surgery, anaesthetise her, and then clean up those wounds. She allowed me to pick her up like a pet dog and even, without resistance, put her into one of my carrying baskets. So far, so good.

At the surgery she was just as friendly as I picked her out and tickled her chest. She was like a pet dog – that is, until she saw the vet advancing brandishing a bandage with which to muzzle her. Normally with a wild badger I would hold it securely by the scruff or with my 'grasper' until its jaws were firmly tied. But this was nice Becky, who loved being held and cuddled. There was no need for such strong-arm tactics here – I did not realise how naïve I was to expect a friendly, willing response in such an unnatural situation. Becky took one look at the vet advancing towards her and in an instant turned into writhing, snarling, snapping 10 kilograms of badger. I saw it coming and moved fast, but not as fast, it seemed, as Becky, who

RIGHT *Bambi and Fate grew up at the Hospital.*

latched her fearsome jaws onto the side of my hand. The pain was excruciating but I still maintained some modicum of pride by not letting go of her and getting her safely back into the basket.

My hand was bleeding quite badly and although I thoroughly rinsed it under the tap and in disinfectant it needed some medical attention.

The vet wrapped it in a temporary dressing and we proceeded to treat Becky's wounds. However, now I handled her as I would a wild badger, and the operation was completed without further trauma.

After I had taken her back to the Hospital to recover from the anaesthetic, I went to Stoke Mandeville Hospital's casualty department. I remember going there when I was kicked in the jaw by a deer, but this time I really had them dumb-founded, with a left hand mangled by a squirrel and the right one torn open by a badger. They must wonder what on earth I get up to.

Something very constructive came out of that visit to Stoke Mandeville for rather than stitching up the badger bite the Sister used small sticky strips of paper specially made for treating that type of wound. They would be ideal for holding together the long tears in the membranes of bats' wings which we had previously found difficult to suture.

Apart from the bite scar, I have one more souvenir of Stoke Mandeville Hospital which gives me a good feeling every time I handle it.

It's nothing very exotic – just an old key ring, but one that says 'Animal House'. It was given to me when the Hospital's stock of animals for laboratory tests was finally disbanded.

I eventually returned Becky to Sally's farm, where she renewed acquaintance with her barn and her favourite paper sack. She still went on nightly excursions and on more than one occasion suffered more bite wounds. However, she soon recovered and gradually stayed out for longer and longer periods.

One morning after a whole week's absence Sally went towards her only to be greeted by snarling teeth and growling. What on earth could be wrong this time? Sally backed off but then jumped – who wouldn't? – as another badger grasped her leg from behind. It whickered. This was Becky, but who was the first badger? When Sally had given her a pat of welcome, Becky let go and then went over to the other badger and they snuffled together. Becky had found herself a beau after all these months of venturing into the wild.

They did not stay in the barn or, as Sally had hoped, set up home in the barn, but instead moved into a sett at the end of the drive where Sally could leave for them, every night, Becky's favourite tit-bits of a Mars bar, a Milky Way and some raisins. Come the spring, there was the pitter patter of tiny paws. Becky and her Beau had two beautiful cubs. Then tragedy struck: Beau was killed on the road at the bottom of the drive and two months later Becky suffered the same fate. Happily, with Sally's help, the two cubs prospered and are still in the sett, coming out at night for their treats of chocolate and raisins.

Before the incident with Becky, in all my years of taking in and handling wild animals I had been bitten only twice before and both times by Chestnut. Now I had doubled that score in just one day.

There are varying degrees of bites that the unprepared can expect from wild animals. I described earlier how Patches, the hedgehog, could give a powerful bite but not inflict a great deal of damage. Foxes have a slashing bite not unlike the slashing of muntjac deer's tusks. Badger's jaws, on the other hand, can be opened only by breaking them, and an otter can easily remove a few fingers. Seals have probably the most dangerous bite of any wild animal in this country – they are said to be able to remove an unwary hand given half the chance.

Basically, however, all wildlife care is a mixture of common sense and experience backed with infinite patience and at times, as when handling a dangerous animal, with intense concentration. Our experience probably paid off when Beatrice Brinkler phoned from Ullapool in the far north of Scotland about a badly injured otter she had taken in. Going back to first principles we were able to advise her how to cope with the otter's head injury even though the Hospital had never handled an otter and some months later it had recovered enough to be released into the sea off the west coast of Scotland.

Handling a sick squirrel is very tricky. It's ferocity and tough skin make it twice as difficult to inject as any other animal, except perhaps a deer, whose skin is extremely thick. Many of the squirrels need fluid injections or antibiotics and I now use a much thinner needle which seems to cause less discomfort. I think that if I had used a larger needle on Nutkin, who had to have three or four courses of antibiotics, he would have ended up like a sieve.

Nutkin had more problems at one time than nearly any other animal I have encountered. He was a true Londoner, found not long after he was born, whimpering under a tree in Regent's Park. A good Samaritan picked him up and took him into London Zoo where Anne Hopkinson looked after him for a while before bringing him up to us.

He had received some sort of severe blow to the head, causing his eyes to swell and bulge outwards grotesquely. There was no way of knowing what permanent injury there was or if in fact his blindness was temporary. All we knew was that there was a young squirrel lost and alone and for the moment anyway quite incapable of looking after himself.

My experience with sightless mammals has been that, although they can never be released, once they have become familiar with the surroundings of their pen they manage quite adequately. Nutkin got the measure of his large cage and was soon nimbly running up and down the numerous branches and actually behaving like a squirrel, burying little caches of

Nutkin had to be held gently but firmly.

peanuts all over the bark litter that was on his floor. He had everything he wanted in the way of peanuts, apples, pears, pine nuts and chocolate digestive biscuits, with plenty of company from anybody who went past his cage. Nobody could resist talking to him.

Then something started to go inexplicably wrong. He stopped eating and instead of scrabbling and playing all day among his branches, he remained hidden away in his nest box. For the first time since he had been with us I donned a thick welding glove and picked him out. He appeared to have a slight swelling to the right side of his little snub nose. It did not appear very important but was obviously very sore – he swore horribly as I touched it. For the moment I found him a place in intensive care although he was obviously quite lost and afraid in a new antiseptic hospital cage.

The swelling grew larger and larger, getting worryingly close to the two top incisors which are so crucial in a squirrel. As soon as I had taken him into intensive care, I had started him on a course of antibiotics. But squirrels need restraining with thick gloves and scream even though you do not hurt them, and Nutkin with this treatment was getting more and more nervous, with the swelling causing obvious agony as he tried to eat.

It showed no signs of receding so we decided to investigate its cause. This necessitated an anaesthetic which at least brought him some temporary relief from the pain. Once he was fast asleep, a sterile needle injected into the swelling released the first pinprick of pus from what turned out to be a massive abscess which must have been causing excruciating pain. We didn't have to decide how to lance the abscess, for as I opened his mouth to see whether it was affecting his teeth, the thing burst inwards, flooding his mouth with its awfulness. I swabbed it all out and the swelling subsided. I hoped that that was the end of it, but abscesses have a nasty habit of re-forming. We would still carry on with the antibiotics, just in case.

Nutkin's improvement, when he came round from anaesthetic, was astounding – he immediately started tucking in to half a digestive biscuit, which was nearly as big as he was as he held it up in his two front paws. However our relief proved to be short lived and two days later another swelling slowly appeared on his lower jaw. It was a second abscess, and when that one was drained, a third formed on his top jaw and the original one started to swell up again.

By this time Nutkin, understandably, was getting paranoid at being constantly manhandled and in true squirrel fashion would swear vehemently at any intrusion into his cage. Frightened stiff, he would challenge the intruder's hand, but instead of biting like any other squirrel he would punch blindly with his little forefeet. I talked to him for ages to try to make friends again. I offered him slices of pear and biscuit so that he would recognise the scent of my hand, although I was just as nervous as he was, pulling my hand out at the slightest movement. Even though I knew that his left and right hooks could never be a problem it took almost a week to train myself to leave my hand there as he attacked it. But at no time during this period did he make any attempt to bite, and this in itself gave me cause for concern.

Had that original abscess caused any damage to those top teeth? I had noticed that even when he nibbled at biscuits he used only his bottom teeth. I would have to pay close attention to Chestnut to see how he nibbled. But I did not have to bother, as soon Nutkin's right top incisor seemed to twist and then it simply fell out. He now had a more serious disability than his questionable eyesight. Squirrels are rodents and rodents' teeth grow constantly, relying on continual gnawing of hard material such as wood and friction with the opposing incisors to keep them trimmed. Presumably Nutkin's lower right incisor would now grow out of control and need regular clipping. He obviously could never survive in the wild but could he even manage to eat in captivity?

With true wildlife resilience Nutkin soon adapted to his new disability and as no more abscesses have appeared he now lives in a much larger cage, though still in intensive care. He has a large log on which he loves to play and he has built a nest in the darkest corner – he is even at last starting to get some sight in those eyes. After first losing the tooth he lived on oranges, soft pears, apples, and chocolate digestives, which he spent hours nibbling the chocolate off, and he now eats monkey nuts, if we remove the shells for him. He still comes at me fists flailing, but he is generally more settled. At least he does not have the pain of those abscesses any more and his teeth are maintaining their own length without my intervention.

It amazes me how foresters throughout Britain persecute the grey squirrel. I think at this juncture I should point out that, contrary to public opinion, the grey squirrel has NOT driven out the native red squirrel. I put it into a nutshell: the reds have been slowly decreasing naturally since the turn of the century. The greys are more resilient animals and have learnt to cope with the virtual desert for wildlife that man

has created in Britain. The grey has learnt to exploit any niche available to it, whereas the reds find it difficult to adjust to change.

I am not saying that squirrels do not damage trees. Mind you, the damage is not half as bad as it's made out to be. However, facts are showing that no matter how many squirrels you kill, Mother Nature and her natural balancing take over, producing more to fill the vacuum. Could it be that shooting squirrels, a practice rife in the countryside, is just an excuse to shoot?

A far more insidious problem is evolving from the lust to shoot. Children see their elders and betters(?) shooting squirrels and they emulate them. Just yesterday we X-rayed a paralysed squirrel to find that it had an air gun pellet shattering its spine. It must have dragged itself around for days before somebody brought it to us, and for once we put an animal out of its genuine misery.

We are not allowed to release grey squirrels because they are not an indigenous species. This is the law being an ass again. Every year pheasants, another non-indigenous species, are released in their thousands. To make matters worse, millions of our indigenous predators, such as foxes, weasels, stoats, owls and even hedgehogs and badgers, are slaughtered to give the foreigners the best chance of survival – though it's not really survival, for the pheasants are destined, before they are many months old, to be blasted full of lead pellets.

RIGHT *The squirrel was trapped at the top of a hollow post.*

Sometimes we are lucky and can free a squirrel from its predicament without having to bring it back to the Hospital. This morning I was called to one at a school in Waddesdon, just 8 kilometres from Aylesbury. The squirrel had apparently got its head and upper body stuck in the top of a hollow square post which supported a wire fence around a tennis court. I borrowed a very high step ladder and, donning my welder's gloves, climbed up to him. Actually he turned out not to be stuck, but his front legs inside the pipe could find no purchase to push himself out, and he did not have strong enough stomach muscles to pull himself back. I just had to lift him free. Needless to say, he bit my gloves, but then he dived between my legs and under a school building. He obviously knew where he was and I could see that he was not injured, so I left him to it.

4 Decisions on Deer

Thankfully there are no problems with releasing most of our patients, as long as extreme care is taken that the animal has a good chance of survival and that it is not going to be a nuisance to anybody. Imagine the wrath we would incite if we were to release rabbits or pheasants into a field of corn or let a heron fly languidly away to a nearby trout farm.

All wild animals have an uphill task trying to eke out an existence from our impoverished countryside. I see our purpose in life as trying to make sure that they are released where they have the best possible chance of survival and the least possible chance of interference from man – although we do prefer hedgehogs to be released into gardens, where the proximity of humans is a definite advantage.

One of our safest release sites for many species is the Wormsley Estate, near High Wycombe. Here Mr Paul Getty has transformed 3,500 acres of parkland into a conservation area, including a deer park and man-made lake. The vast woodland areas are now being managed and are home to many badgers, and fallow and muntjac deer. Any trees lost are being replaced with native species of a true Saxon mix that would have featured in Britain in the fifth and sixth centuries. We take very great care and release selected species only after lengthy discussions with the estate managers. In a delicate ecological balance like this, where woodland and hedgerows are very young, we would be foolish to release animals which might damage the crucial growing tips of the new recolonising plants.

We first came to know the staff on the Wormsley Estate over a very tragic deer fawn casualty. The estate has a number of footpaths passing through it. By one of these, two walkers came across a beautiful male fallow fawn hanging by his back legs from the top of a wire fence. It appeared that the fawn had been following his mother in jumping over the fence but had caught his hind legs.

Their flight over the lethal barrier may have been caused by the perennial problem on the estate of people allowing their dogs to run free. Any dog will chase a deer, with horrifying consequences – some pets will even severely bite the wild animal's hocks. There is a constant

The little fallow deer soon settled with the female muntjac.

campaign at Wormsley to ask people to keep their dogs on leads, a practice I would like to see adopted wherever there are deer at liberty.

I called the vet to look at the deer's hind legs. What he told us gave us cause for concern – the legs were not broken but there was a chance that the wire strands had irrevocably damaged the blood supply to both hooves. Deer have very little flesh on the lower part of their legs, so gangrene is always a distinct possibility.

The little fallow deer with his large ears, saucer eyes and handsomely dappled coat soon settled with a female muntjac we had at St Tiggywinkles. He fed well and could walk on those two legs but gradually there was the telltale spreading of blackness from the hooves upwards. As he walked the hooves seemed to bend forward at a crazy angle. I knew what was happening and called in the vet to confirm the worst. As I held the fawn in my arms he nuzzled my ear with his big wet nose. The vet checked the feet and on seeing the black brittle husks agreed with me. We knew that euthanasia was the only option. Deer cannot possibly be asked to continue with two feet missing – so much pressure is exerted on their hooves that any exposed stump would be permanently red raw.

Deer fawns are definitely favourites of most people, and the vet admitted that it was the most heart-rending task he had ever had to carry out. I cuddled the fawn to me once more as the vet inserted the fatal injection into his vein. Slowly and peacefully the fawn's head sagged onto my shoulder. He was dead.

The deer could not possibly continue . . .

Some people think that looking after animals is all caressing and cooing. Well it's not. Sometimes you have to make this kind of decision which, believe me, takes every ounce of resolve you have in your body.

In my book *Something in a Cardboard Box*, the two muntjac deer Mistletoe and Costly lifted us out of gloom. Now I was asking them to do it again.

When the unfortunate fallow fawn was brought into the Hospital, Gavin Jones, who looks after the deer on the Wormsley Estate, phoned throughout his stay, deeply concerned about his plight. In fact because of the hazard

created by the wire on top of the fences Gavin arranged to have it all removed – miles and miles of it. Gavin had a very keen interest in muntjac deer and offered to build a large enclosure for any which were permanently disabled and might need a home. Of course, Mistletoe and Costly were still prancing about the Hospital and, as neither could ever be released, we quickly took him up on the offer.

Getting them over to Wormsley was fraught with problems but with sedatives and Andy controlling them we managed it without injuries either to them or us. We also took over, for release, a rarity for our part of Britain – a roe deer fawn, christened Daisy for the delicate nature of her demeanour, quite unlike the two boisterous muntjacs. All these had lived together for a while and so knew each other well, which was an asset as they settled in. Costly and Mistletoe loved their new pen. They ran up and down at breakneck speed, turning in an instant at the end of each dash until they were both gasping for breath. Daisy took it all in her stride, standing watching the two gambolling muntjac as if to say, 'What's all the fuss about? It's only a pen.'

Gavin's daughter Marie had a great love of animals and with hour after hour of patience she had all three coming to her hand for tit-bits, pieces of apple, and also pear, the supreme favourite of all muntjac.

There were two freshly constructed lakes on the site upon which we wanted to release three coots that we had hand-reared. As we first let them go on the beach, they promptly turned round and walked back to us. I suppose they had never seen, or could not remember seeing, a stretch of water larger than their washing-up bowl swimming pool back at the Hospital. After about a half an hour's cajoling they eventually took reluctantly to their natural element, but certainly not like ducks, or should I say coots, to water.

Far less reluctant to go were the pair of barn owls which featured in another release project on the Estate. We have had, over the years, considerable experience in reintroducing barn

RIGHT *Two barn owls ready to be released.*

owls, the white ghost owls which so often feature in horror movies. In spite of new ideas on the release of barn owls, we have always found our scheme of wiring up an old barn, to contain the birds for the winter, and then releasing them when they have chicks in early summer is very successful. Our first project, way back in 1984, when we placed a pair of owls in a barn in London, was so successful that in June 1985 the two adults and their five young were released, to be the first barn owls in London for over forty years. And they are still in the area, although one has since drowned in a horse trough during a fight with a cat.

The pair of barn owls, in the specially secluded part of the barn at Wormsley, did breed during their first season together. However once they were released they adopted their tragic barn owl habit of destroying their own young. The pair are now resident on Wormsley and we hope to put another pair in another barn soon, as the open fields and hedgerows on the Estate appear to be ideal barn owl territory.

While we were monitoring the progress of the owls, Gavin found another fallow fawn caught in a section of wire fence that had not yet been altered. By the time I arrived he had the deer under a heat lamp in his barn. It was a tiny little female deer with, it seemed, even bigger eyes and ears than the last one. As Gavin lifted her out I quickly checked the damage to her legs. It was a similar injury to that of the young buck, but at least it was only to one leg. Although Gavin wanted to look after her, I felt a vet

should see the leg. It would definitely need a course of medical treatment. We drove back home with Twiggy – she really was a small deer – cuddled on Sue's lap. The vet came to look at the leg and gave, unfortunately, the same prognosis as for the other fallow fawn. We would have to wait and see.

For a week we watched Twiggy pine on her blanket at the corner of the lawn. There was still hope that maybe she could go back to her mother, so we kept our contact with her to a minimum. However, the foot gradually turned black, and then the lower part of the leg – it was slowly dying upwards. Neither Sue nor I could face the prospect of having to put her down: she was very young – young enough to be tamed and settled into a life of captivity. But the leg would have to be amputated if she was to have any chance of survival. From now on she would always live with people in a confined home so the sooner she got used to it the better. That is, if she survived the operation.

We had operated on many deer and had almost become used to their shenanigans under anaesthetic. Twiggy was no exception but where she outdid Fate, the previous deer amputee still living on Sally's farm who had taken days to stand up, was in standing up on her three little spindly legs the moment the anaesthetic wore off. We did not need to use the sling arrangement, a hammock made from an old blanket, that had helped both Bambi and Fate

Twiggy, the fallow fawn.

get over their traumas by keeping their weight off their legs. Twiggy soon settled to live at the Hospital and within weeks was fit enough to be taken to join Mistletoe and Costly at Wormsley.

We had already adapted the sling system to suit birds and now I was using it with a fox with a fractured sacrum (where the pelvis joins the spine) which would benefit from a similar form of traction. The fox soon settled in the sling and looked comfortable, but as soon as my back was turned it ate the straps, webbing and Vet-bed that supported him. Finding him on the floor, I refitted him with a new sling, which he promptly ate. After the third failure, I gave up – he would have to recover in a cage where he could eat only his expensive Vet-bed. (Vet-beds are specially made of a lambswool-type material that allows fluid through, keeping the animal dry.)

Somehow a fox seems so self-confident compared with the skittish panic that is a deer. We treat a great many muntjac and have at least conquered most of their idiosyncracies, not with sedatives but with steroids. We have found that one good injection with dexamethasone, backed with antibiotics, will save many DTAs (victims of Deer Traffic Accidents). We have only so far taken in two Chinese water deer, another immigrant species which escaped the zoos to colonise the British countryside. The first was one of those snub-nosed fawns which draw out all of Sue's mothering instincts. The second was an

The fox looked comfortable and seemed settled...

adult DTA with a broken jaw and the general lethargy caused by concussion.

Chinese water deer are the only deer species in Europe that do not grow antlers. Instead the males grow very sharp tusks which protrude from the top jaw, very like a muntjac's tusks but much longer. The deer we took in was fortunately a doe. Her concussion caused her to stand completely oblivious of her surroundings, which was probably a good thing as she did not get frightened. Her pelage was quite stiff and wiry compared with other species I had handled and was generally the colour of an old-fashioned teddy bear.

Her broken jaw was quite badly swollen. She was unable to eat at all so for two weeks I kept her alive on Complan and Lectade which she guzzled down if I pushed her nose into the mixture. The vet could do nothing to fix the broken jaw – it was another case where we would have to 'wait and see'. However she never gave us the chance and that Sunday morning died. Perhaps the Complan diet was not rich enough for her requirements. I am now using an American substitute food called Ensure. It's primarily used for humans with throat problems who cannot eat solid food. So far I have found it very successful with badgers and foxes, and if another deer problem crops up I feel that I stand more chance of dealing with it.

Christmas Day for Sue and me is just a normal working day except for the fact that none of the other helpers come in to the

Hospital. We are prepared to receive any casualties, but must admit to giving the in-patients for once only a cursory cleaning before feeding them all. As people tend to stay at home at Christmas there is less chance of casualties being found, though there are normally a few sparrows or blackbirds caught by cats and a memorable Christmas robin the year before last. This year Christmas Day started at four o'clock in the morning when a frantic buzzing on our raucous door bell got us out of bed. At the door were John and Audrey Eustace, friends who live on the Champneys Estate near Tring. John was quite upset and led me to the boot of his car. It was just as well it was a large car for filling it was a massive fallow buck. John had seen it lying in the road in Ashridge Forest, the best area for fallow deer near to us. He had stopped and was comforting the deer when another car approached at high speed. Franti-cally John waved it down but it just kept coming so that at the last moment John had to jump out of the way as the car went right over the deer. Obviously the deer suffered even more injury and although John managed to get it into his car it was dead on arrival at the Hospital. This road through Ashridge is a fast main road and a death trap for the many deer which live in the forest. It's a pity a speed limit is not imposed or reflectors fitted to the roadside to deflect the headlights sideways so that they warn deer of approaching vehicles.

The adult Chinese water deer.

There is now a gadget on the market called 'Animal Alert'. When mounted on the bumper of a car it is supposed to send out a high fre-quency signal that warns all animals of the approaching car. We have fitted them to mine and Andy's cars to try them out but as yet have had no opportunity to test them – or perhaps, having seen no animals on the road in front of the cars, they are in fact working? They may well be the answer to badger and hedgehog accidents and save a lot of pain and suffering.

At the other end of that Christmas Day I took another deer call, this time round about mid-night. Another deer, a muntjac, had been hit by a car near to the Wootton House Estate about 12 kilometres west of Aylesbury. It had appar-ently managed to drag itself into thick under-growth by the side of the road and could not be retrieved by the driver. Knowing the problems of cornering and capturing deer I summoned Andy from his Christmas revels to give me a hand.

Andy never complains whatever hour I call him out – he is always over within minutes and raring to go. On this Christmas night he had his best togs on, but this did not bother him either.

It did not even bother him as we had to crawl on all fours into the thick thorn undergrowth. We spotted the deer sitting dazed but quiet in a small clearing. The strategy we adopted was one we'd used many times before. I cut off its escape route by crawling in a big circle and taking up position behind it. Then we closed in from both sides, either of us prepared to grab

The wild rabbit used to sleep next to Doofer.

the deer at the first opportunity.

Andy got him first and held on for all he was worth until I could reach him. We could not stand up in the thick thorn so we had to crawl back to the road with the bucking deer between us. Andy's clothes were ruined but he did not seem to mind. He was glad that we had caught the deer which, from the look at its condition, would need only a couple of days at the Hospital to recover all its faculties.

We have only one deer at St Tiggywinkles at the moment – another muntjac buck – although a vet has just phoned me from Ware to say that another is on its way to us after being savaged by dogs. The deer now with us – Andy's wife Dot, another volunteer at the Hospital, calls him 'Doofer' – had an injury that nobody had ever seen before. Trapped in a concrete enclosure, an electricity board sub-station or something of the sort, his efforts to escape succeeded in wearing his hooves completely away. The feet were clean and uninfected and as nobody can tell me whether hooves will grow again I am keeping Doofer alive to give him a chance to recover. He sits in his pen quite docile and unaffected by the hustle and bustle of the Hospital. He eats, can walk well on a soft floor of hay and, most important, does not appear stressed in captivity. He has two wild rabbits living in with him and I am reasonably confident that eventually, although it's going to be a long time, his hooves will recover enough so that he can be released. I know his deer sure-footedness will prevent him treading on one of his pen mates.

5 The Year of the Fox

It's funny, but neither Sally nor Gavin are happy to let me release foxes on their land. Consequently, I have to find somewhere else to release them, as far from hunting areas as possible, and often this will be on territory unfamiliar to them and me. That's one thing about this work with animals that can keep me awake at night: the thought that one of the released foxes may roam into hunting territory and be tortured to death in the horrifying ritual of the bloody coats and hunting horns. Just imagine cutting the face of a living or recently dead fox and wiping the blood around the faces of your children. That's just one of the disgusting rituals practised by huntsmen in the name of tradition. It makes my blood run cold just to think of the way that the fox suffers for 'sport'.

During this last year we have taken in more foxes than ever before. I have been fortunate enough to meet foxes of all ages and conditions and every one I have had to admire for its sheer grace and wildness. In previous years I attributed the lack of fox casualties to their acuity in avoiding being hit by vehicles. Somehow this year has seen a deterioration in their kerb drill and a regular influx of casualties, resulting in our treating four or five foxes at any one time during the year.

I don't think that the increase in fox casualties means there are more foxes or that there is less hunting. In fact it has been proven that fox-hunting has little or no effect on fox numbers – there goes another hunt argument out of the window. The reason for the increase is still a mystery, but could it be that, like many other species, foxes are moving from the blandness of the countryside into the towns, where food is plentiful but the road traffic is heavier?

Any kind of confinement is purgatory to a fox, and I appreciate that the small areas at Pemberton Close are especially restrictive. There is also the added concern when caring for foxes of the ripeness of their typical aroma. Do not get me wrong, the scent is not particularly unpleasant – in fact it's heaven on earth to a fox of the opposite sex – it's just that it's far stronger than any other smell, including the very expensive

The water butt contained 3 inches of sludge and a tiny fox cub.

Parvocide we use as a disinfectant. At the beginning of the year the scent seems to hang in the air. Walk through any wood in January and you can tell where Fox has been doing his courting.

At Pemberton Close I try to be very careful to avoid nuisance to the neighbours. In fact none of our patients makes a lot of noise so that is never a problem and Parvocide soon clears the after-effects of swans and badgers. Foxes are a different problem, but there I rely on Nigel and Sharon Brock, our neighbours. True, they are staunch Trust supporters, but they are open enough to tell me if they smell anything amiss. It will be great at the new Hospital where the wide open spaces will make things so much easier.

Back to our foxy year, this started with the perennial problem of orphaned, or supposedly orphaned, cubs. In the same way that we campaign to leave baby birds alone, we are forever advising, 'Leave the cub alone. The vixen will soon round up one which has strayed.' Our whole aproach is graphically illustrated by a rescue call I had to make in Rickmansworth. In a large, very overgrown garden in a residential part of town a vixen was apparently raising a family under an old shed. Next to a decrepit greenhouse was a pile of logs, a tempting stairway for a young adventurous fox cub up to the top of a rainwater barrel. I can hear you gasp in horror but luckily the barrel was as full of holes as the greenhouse. Instead of water it contained a few centimetres of sludge and old leaves, and a tiny cub mewing for its mother. I reached in to lift it out and it snapped and spat – marvellous spirit in an animal no larger than a kitten. I did not fancy having it clamped onto my finger with its needle-sharp teeth, so I used my badger stick to deflect its jaws while I lifted it clear, as I would do with an adult fox. Even though it was soaked through, its spirit never dampened, as time and again it spat at me in defiance. I gave it a quick rub down, and then put it down near the entrance to the nursery under the shed. It knew immediately where it was and called softly for its mother as it ran back underneath. Needless to say I covered the top of the rain barrel to make sure that another animal would not fall in.

This mother was very much alive. It's only when we know that a vixen has been killed that we intervene and take over her maternal duties. This was the case with the five fox cubs that were brought to us shortly after the rain barrel incident. Tiny cubs do not look a bit like foxes. In fact, they have the appearance of dusky-coloured kittens, and many people find it hard to identify them. The foster family where we sent these cubs had great experience of raising cubs of all ages. Being 'farmed out', they stood a much better chance of growing up still wild than if they had been confined in the hurly-burly of the Hospital.

That, in a nutshell, is the major problem in rearing fox cubs. They are so easy to tame, but a tame fox is a poor relation of the wild animal

Noddy with a feather on his nose – he would play like any other fox cub.

and somehow always has that yearning for wild places haunting its eyes. Quite a few people think that it's a good idea to have a pet fox. Yes, it is a beautiful animal, arguably more intelligent than a faithful dog, but as soon as it is about six months old it becomes nocturnal, very agile and destructive, and has that aromatic fox scent. Each summer, every animal welfare centre or sanctuary is plagued with calls from frantic people whose pet fox cubs have turned into destructive animals of the night. Welfare groups can take only so many, and I am afraid that other would-be pet owners are stuck with their mistake with nobody but themselves to blame.

It's to try to avoid this kind of situation that we go over the top in saying 'leave fox cubs alone'. However, if there is something wrong with a cub we will dive to the rescue without a moment's hesitation. Spitz was the first genuine fox cub casualty of the year. He had been found wandering well away from any fox territory and one look at his eyes told that something was not quite right. Instead of the usual dark eyes of a young fox, Spitz's eyes were light blue in colour, pale and opaque, as though he were blind. But he could see, if not too well, and soon took on anyone who went near him – hence his name.

On close examination the vet could see no signs of traumatic injury to the eyes and felt that Spitz could see fairly well; he could probably be released once he had grown up. On his own, Spitz moped quite a bit, but he brightened considerably when we introduced a playmate, our next genuine fox cub casualty, Noddy.

'Noddy' was another of the infamous, silly, but affectionate names we give to some of our patients. The poor little fox cub had what is known in the animal welfare world as an intention tremor, where every passing thought caused his little head to nod exactly like those toy dogs seen in the backs of cars. He was a friendly little fellow who we knew from the start could never be released, and so could be pampered and petted. The vet diagnosed cerebral hyperplasia, possibly the result of the cub's mother suffering an infection while she was pregnant. This not unusual congenital condition was further confirmed by Noddy's other symptoms: he could not walk properly, tending to move both his back legs in a hopping sort of gait, and the toes on his back legs were not properly separated. The prognosis was poor but, for the moment, Noddy appeared not to be in distress. In fact he played rough-and-tumble with Spitz perfectly normally. It was only the nodding head and peculiar gait that gave any indication of his affliction.

And then Maisie, another genuine orphan, joined our crèche, and the three became inseparable. They had become a family. We moved them all together to Surrey, where we knew their foster mother would lavish attention on them and gradually get Spitz and Maisie back to the wild. Unfortunately Noddy was on borrowed time and when he started to suffer fits we decided to call it a day to prevent him suffering unnecessarily. He had lived for a few

The dog fox begins to recover from his operation.

happy months and there had been the chance that he might have coped. At least we tried.

Spitz, who could now see very well in spite of his funny-coloured eyes, and Maisie were released in the autumn and for a long time visited at night for tit-bits.

With a severely disabled animal like Noddy, less set in its ways than adults, we always give it a chance to see if it will accept life in captivity. Each animal is different. Each is an individual who will react independently to given situations and stresses. One vixen, who had to have a front leg amputated, has settled so well in her foster home in Hertfordshire that she now herself fosters orphaned cubs and has had some of her own through a resident dog fox – a success story.

Foxes are usually very adaptable and respond well to treatment. This year not only have we had resounding successes with mange cases, but also our vet has been able to carry out quite complicated orthopaedic operations. I am just about to release a large dog fox who had snapped the cruciate ligament of one of his back legs. In a very skilled operation, the vet drilled into two of the major leg bones and then

installed a temporary artificial tendon, made from a narrow strip of skin cut from the incision site, to last until the existing joint was fully functional again.

Another fox who underwent a tricky operation and who is now coming up for release is a vixen with a stainless steel plate holding a fractured humerus in one of her front legs. With hedgehogs we have always let fractured humeri heal spontaneously. After assisting at this fox operation I can see why. It all sounds very easy – open up the leg, drill the screwholes, fix the plate and then stitch up – until you realise that the radial nerve, which must not be damaged, runs right across the operation site. It's hard enough keeping a fox's radial nerve out of the way but the smallness of a hedgehog would make it nearly impossible to plate the humerus – that is, even if you could get a plate small enough for the job. Mind you, I am sure that as the Teaching Hospital develops there will come a time when we have orthopaedic equipment and accessories specifically made for those intricate operations on the smaller animals.

The sheer tenacity of a wild animal as it hangs on to life, and its ability to conquer even the most severe discomfort and infection make every casualty worth trying to save. A broken leg will disable a man for months on end, and if infected will make survival very difficult. A fox just shrugs off this kind of impairment and only succumbs to capture when the infection has

Feeling himself again, the dog fox is nearly ready to go.

generally debilitated its whole metabolism.

JR, a male fox, came in with a horribly infected compound fracture of the radius and ulna bones of one of his front legs, and I asked the vet to look at it. With an infected compound fracture the wound has to be kept open to drain and heal. This precludes the use of plaster of Paris to splint the leg or the introduction of any metal parts, which would just let in more infection.

I always think of Robert Jones as a Member of Parliament who is strong on animal issues. However, I wonder whether he is aware of a system of bandaging known throughout the world as the Robert Jones Bandage. The vet recommended this treatment for the fox's leg and as the bandage consisted, among other tapes and things, of 75 per cent of a roll of cotton wool, you can imagine how the bandaged leg appeared almost as large as the rest of the fox put together.

We continued the treatment by changing the Robert Jones regularly and, miraculously, within three weeks the leg was healed. Soon afterwards the fox was returned to his domain in High Wycombe.

Quite a lot of people are pleased to see foxes in and around their gardens. The slander that they are vermin has now, thankfully, nearly sunk into history. There are, however, some ignorant people who still think that foxes are dirty, which reminds me of a protracted incident at a local hospital for the mentally handicapped.

As part of their occupational therapy some of

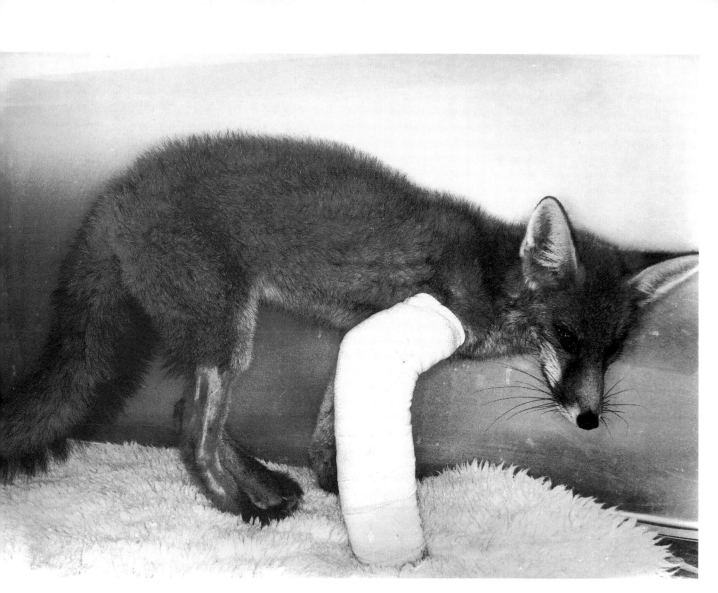

A typical Robert Jones Bandage.

the patients pack items for the nearby Stoke Mandeville Hospital. The building then used as their workshop was a prefabricated structure set about 30 centimetres off the ground. The gap below the building had been almost totally enclosed by boarding. However a local vixen, as quick as any fox to exploit man's shortcomings, had found a gap and moved into the wonderful dry, draught-free den under the toilets near the entrance to the building. The patients at the hospital loved to be able to watch the coming and going of the vixen to her eight cubs but the 'powers that be' decided they would have to go and called in the pest control man. Now the law in all its inanity has given pest controllers *carte blanche* to kill animals which are not specifically on the protected list. By this criterion, most of our mammal species can be classed as pests.

Luckily, the lady who ran the OT unit liked the foxes and asked for a stay of execution for a week so that they might be moved. She called the RSPCA, who called us.

Nigel, Andy and I went along to the hospital to assess the situation. It was impossible to reach the family of foxes but we could quite clearly see the eight cubs running about under the building. More often than not a vixen will have an alternative nest site, and so our strategy was to try and get her to move her family out herself.

Night after night, all that week, we were at the hospital putting down all manner of fox repellents to try to get her to move. They didn't work; the hospital now smelt of the repellents,

Three RSPCA inspectors rounding up the fox cubs flushed from under the hospital building.

and the fox stayed put. Graham Cornick, a fox expert, told me that foxes just cannot tolerate Jeyes Fluid, so down that went onto the surrounding area – litres of it. Still the vixen would not move. Jokingly, I said to the RSPCA Inspector, 'The only way to move those fox cubs is to get the fire brigade to hose them out!'

'Do that,' said the Inspector, 'and I'll do you all for cruelty.'

Our main hope of a reprieve was that the pest controllers would not be able to get at the foxes, or be able to shoot them in such a confined space, but I could not think of a real answer.

The day before the deadline I had to go to London to see my publisher. I still had to earn a living and the foxes were in no danger that day. As I drove out of town I called in at the hospital to leave a cage trap, which would not harm the vixen or cubs, as a last hope. I was met by more RSPCA inspectors in one place than had been

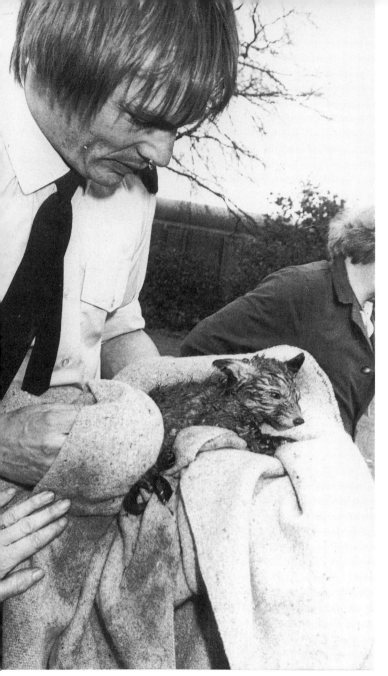

seen since four of them tried to catch an elusive terrapin in the Sid Jenkins television series. Apparently the RSPCA had, after all, called in the fire brigade.

I could not bear to watch and went off to London. Splashed all over the local papers a week later were the pictures of the cubs being flushed out and caught. All's well that ends well – or is it? The eight cubs were successfully hand-raised by an animal welfare group and have now been released in National Trust property (not I hope on National Trust land where hunting is allowed). But the vixen, cubless, no doubt wandered that part of town for some time to come.

I do not condemn the RSPCA for their methods on this occasion. Dealing with wildlife is often a question of improvisation and initiative with the two bodies working side by side.

RSPCA inspector Alan Brockbank drying one of the cubs.

6 Seals, Rabbits and Hedgehogs

Over the years we have broken much new ground, and we have planned to publish our findings – and our revelations – and to give lectures when the new Teaching Hospital, St Tiggywinkles, is officially opened in 1991. As a result of our constant campaigning to try to save injured wildlife, we are all the time receiving more and more requests to go public and to provide further information to a Britain intent on saving its wild animals.

Our most spectacular early success was our breakthrough in rearing orphaned hedgehogs. You perhaps would not think that many people would be interested in the right mix of goats' milk and colostrum, or the terrors of toileting a live pin cushion, but they were. The few who took in animals in their spare time were not the only devotees. The veterinary profession were also avidly interested and asked me to give a paper to the prestigious British Veterinary Zoological Society at their Annual General Meeting held at London Zoo. Another talk followed soon afterwards, this time to the Association of British Wild Animal Keepers at Twycross Zoo. And then late in 1988 we were

BABY HEDGEHOG EMERGENCY KIT

Heated cage
Pair of tweezers
1 ml syringe
16 g hypodermic needle without a point
1 inch of bicycle valve rubber
Cotton buds
Abidec multivitamin drops
Frozen goat's milk
Frozen goat's colostrum
Small pack of Lectade
Bottle of Savlon

Read *The Complete Hedgehog* for method of rearing orphans

actively involved in running the first symposium of the British Wildlife Rehabilitation Council, which I had set up with Stefan Ormrod of the RSPCA two years before.

I probably see more wildlife casualties than anyone else and yet even for me there were new ideas that cropped up during the day, especially about species that I had not encountered. The one disappointment, not just to me but to many others, was that although Britain was in the throes of an epidemic among its seal populations the paper on 'Diseases of Seals' did not discuss the viruses associated with the so-called Seal Plague.

Being completely land-locked in the dead centre of England I did not expect to get involved with the seal problem. However, when the front page of my *Mail on Sunday* showed an RSPCA Inspector shooting a seal because 'nothing could be done to save the seals and most of them were *in extremis* [dying] anyway', I felt that something had to be done. My opinion is that only a fully trained veterinary surgeon can say whether an animal is *in extremis*. How could anybody standing on a windswept beach ascertain the condition of a seal without even knowing what was wrong with it? Many were said to have clogged-up eyes. Could this not have been simple conjunctivitis? But nobody was bothering to check. I knew, from following the progress of the seal plague, that Lenie t'Hart at the seal hospital in Pieterburen in

Five orphan baby hedgehogs.

Holland had cured some seals but England had not, as yet, even tried.

The research in Holland had identified a canine distemper virus. I had seen vets in the country overcome the dreaded parvovirus which threatened to wipe out our dog population. I was confident that given the opportunity and the encouragement Britain's vets could do something for the seals.

I am fed up with animals being destroyed just because they would be difficult to treat. I had never handled seals, but when I saw that newspaper article I knew that, rather than see them shot, I was willing to have a good try at saving them.

It was Sunday, making it doubly difficult to get anything done, and whatever I planned was bound to cost money, so the first thing I did was to contact my fellow Managing Trustees of the Trust.

Over the years we had slowly, 10p by 10p, accumulated a fund to build the Wildlife Teaching Hospital. My proposal to the Trustees was that £10,000 of this be used to get something off the ground for seals – it might fail dismally, but we had dealt with many 'firsts' at the Hospital and might be able to help a few seals. Our decisions at the Hospital, arrived at with one accord I am glad to say, had always been to put the animal first. This meeting was no different. I was given the go-ahead to set up a rescue network, albeit temporarily, to meet the immediate needs of the seals then coming ashore. If only the new Hospital had been built,

we could have coped right from the start.

Obviously, to anyone who has seen it, our present suburban site at Pemberton Close was not remotely suitable for seals, so my first task was to find somewhere in which to set up quarantine and all the other facilities we would need. The ideal site would be a disused transport depot with space, a concrete floor and ample water facilities to cope with seals. I wanted it to be central, around Aylesbury, both for ease of access and because we would be roughly equidistant from all four coasts.

Councils have a great many transport depots, so even though it was Sunday I phoned Martin Willey, Chief of Technical Services at Aylesbury Vale District Council. A giant of a man with boundless energy and good humour, Martin set about our request immediately and within the hour had found a possible location, an empty vehicle depot in Buckingham about 30 kilometres north of Aylesbury. Of course it would have to go before the Council the following week but for the moment we had our emergency centre.

We then needed a reception centre, at least in Norfolk where most of the seals were coming in. We generally say at the Trust, 'If you want anything out of the ordinary, ask Nigel.'

Nigel Brock, our next-door neighbour, knows somebody everywhere and, lo and behold, had a friend in Norfolk with some land who agreed to be our reception centre.

As they had done in the past, our volunteer helpers offered to drive ambulances to and from Norfolk. (Although this seemed at the time to be the answer, we subsequently found out from colleagues in Holland that carrying seals by road can be detrimental to the animals.) However, it seemed that the whole of Britain was up in arms at the needless slaughter on the beaches and, after a hasty meeting on the Monday afternoon, the shooting was stopped and Norfolk County Council came forward with a vacant transport depot that Greenpeace and the RSPCA could use as a seal centre.

For the moment we could step down. However, the concept of a seal centre attracted

RIGHT *Another crash-landed Manx shearwater.*

a lot of media attention and during a television interview with a representative of Greenpeace we learnt that the centre was only to be run as a temporary measure for six to eight weeks. There were no plans at that time by either party to establish the permanent seal rehabilitation centre that the country so desperately needed, in spite of all the funds the media had generated.

The temporary centre was set up at Docking and when the first seal arrived, not diseased but caught up in fishing nets, pandemonium apparently broke out. We received a call and Sue and I decided to drive up to Norfolk the following day to see if we could do anything to help.

September was bringing our usual crop of crash-landed Manx shearwaters, and since Norfolk has plenty of sea we decided to take the latest arrival with us, for release. I had never been to Norfolk and so headed, by map, for the point where the road came nearest to the sea. 'Snettisham Beach' the sign said, and down the single-track road we drove. A car park, how thoughtful. We paid our 50p, took up the shearwater and climbed the sea wall. There was no sea to be seen. The tide must have been out. There was nothing for it but to take the bird back to the car and release the shearwater on the nearest river estuary.

At last it paddled away and we could head inland for Docking. The scene there was, by now, reasonably under control with much banging of nails and painting making the old depot shipshape. There were still television crews milling around, while in the middle of it all an RSPCA Chief Inspector was sergeant-majoring at all and sundry. Stefan Ormrod and Tim Thomas from RSPCA headquarters brought a little sanity to the place and briefed us on the situation. I was rather concerned about a little common seal isolated in a corner sandbag pen. Its great saucer eyes were sad but full of life. It did not strike me as being ill. In fact, it was the one rescued from fishing nets. I hoped it was going to be released from this draughty barn of a place before somebody brought in a highly contagious seal infected with the virus.

The chief inspector did not seem keen on us staying so Sue and I set off back to Aylesbury. Docking was fine as the temporary measure that Greenpeace intended but something had to be done about a more scientific treatment centre because the disease was not about to disappear after eight weeks.

I desperately wanted to be able to do something to help the coming year's seal pups who would undoubtedly contract the virus. The answer seemed to be to look at the feasibility of including a seal facility at the new St Tiggywinkles along the lines of the Pieterburen hospital. As I sometimes perhaps get a little emotive when it comes to sick animals, I arranged for Ian Mackay, the architect for our new Hospital, and our vet to fly to Holland and examine the possibilities from a more scientific viewpoint.

Lenie t'Hart, and Lies Vedder, the resident veterinary surgeon, were very helpful in supplying vital information about how they worked.

For one thing, they flew their casualty seals to the hospital from all along the Dutch coast, often farther than from Aylesbury to the sea. Also, a vet went out to collect each casualty – a very important point for us to bear in mind.

Yes, it would be feasible for us to treat seals at St Tiggywinkles, and Ian could adjust the plans to include the highly specialised water plant and underfloor heating. Another of our Vice-Presidents, Dennis Furnell, the well-known writer, broadcaster and naturalist, had a full pilot's licence and assured us of the availability of air transport to strips around Aylesbury.

There were many thousands of pounds available to welfare groups at the inception of the seal crisis. We have not relied on any of this money. I only hope that it hasn't all gone down the drain on projects that will not really cope with seal problems.

One thing that came out of all the mayhem concerning the seals was the public and Government demand to find a cure for the seal virus, although prior to 1988 seals were legislated against as pests, and fishermen had certain licence to kill them. Like seals, rabbits are mammals, and myxomatosis is another virus, causing just as much pain and misery as the one that attacks seals. Rabbits, too, are classed as pests, in their case to farmers, and yet there has been no public outcry to search for a cure for the Rabbit Plague. Why not?

Many people think that myxomatosis was a disease of the 1950s and do not realise that its horrors are still very much part of our countryside – we still see many dozens of cases during a year. Though we have always been advised that euthanasia is the only humane treatment, we have been able to take action against the vectors of the disease – rabbit fleas, or biting flies – by thoroughly dusting the sick animal; more often, in the hopelessness of saving the rabbit, we have sprayed the animal and its carrying box with insecticide and then burnt the box. This destroyed any chance that those particular parasites would spread the disease to other rabbits or, very rarely, to hares.

I had always followed blindly the advice I had been given but a chance encounter with two young rabbits on the road between Leicester and Northampton set me, once again, querying the slaughter policy, so easily adopted as a 'cure-all'.

It was at the end of my book-signing tour with *Something in a Cardboard Box*. I had just left an interview at Radio Leicester and was driving through the artificial point-to-point course that is the Leicestershire countryside, thinking to myself that no self-respecting fox would ever willingly live in a landscape so contrived for hunting, when all of a sudden I saw a rabbit on the road. I slowed to a halt, blocking both carriageways, and jumped out, only to see the rabbit, a youngster, disappear into a field of crops. There was another rabbit, a doe, sitting on the verge opposite. She looked to be in trouble and so I approached her slowly from behind. I noticed that she could not see me as her eyes were swollen and closed, the first signs of myxomatosis. I was soon within arm's length of her, and I reached forward and grabbed her firmly around the middle. Picking her up and securely supporting her back end, as rabbits have very weak spines, I tucked her in among all the maps and book paraphernalia in the back of the car and resumed my (now late) journey for a book-signing session in Northampton. Mikki Most, as I called her, did not need anything immediately and could curl up in the car until I got back to Aylesbury.

After the signing session and another radio interview I quickly covered the 80 kilometres back to Aylesbury. I am well aware of the lethal contagiousness of myxomatosis, so initially, on our arrival at the Hospital, Mikki had to be quarantined in the front porch and dusted for fleas. After about an hour, her holding box was destroyed, and she was put safely in a new box for transfer to the first aid unit. There were no other rabbits or hares in the Hospital at that time but I still took precautions in case there was just one flea left alive. Then I had to consider how to go about treating her.

I can imagine the arms going up in horror.

'Fancy treating a myxomatosis rabbit. It should be put down!'

'Why?' I say. 'After all, a wild rabbit is just as much a feeling animal as a tame rabbit or cat. It is of the same class of animals as a seal, and everybody clamours for a cure to be found for their virus diseases.'

Again I can hear the outcry, 'Rabbits are pests.'

But then so, 'they say', are seals to fishing fleets. Everything seems to be a pest to somebody: kingfishers are pests to pond owners; peregrines are pests to pigeon fanciers; even dogs are pests to sheep farmers, and look how quickly the veterinary profession evolved a treatment to cope with the sudden onslaught of canine parvovirus. I am sure that if people put their minds to it they could come up with some form of treatment.

Perhaps we could do something at the new Hospital.

For now, I had a very sick young rabbit whose eyes looked terribly swollen and sore and who would probably much like something to eat and drink. That is the strange thing about myxomatosis – the afflicted rabbit still carries on feeding, drinking and even courting up until the moment of its demise. When people had a virus infection, such as a cold or flu, my opinion has always been that there is no artificial cure, and that we rely entirely on the body's immune system to conquer the disease. What if we were to give Mikki all the support possible? If we just kept her alive, her own bodily defences might have the chance to defeat the invader. However, for now, I interfered with Nature by bathing her eyes open and applying some soothing ophthalmic ointment.

We have in an isolated corner of our intensive care unit a large cage, with a perspex front, known as 'Nigel's Hospital Cage' because our ever-willing next-door neighbour made it for treatment of larger patients. After making

Mikki comfortable in this cage, I turned up the heater and offered her bowls of water and coarse goat mix, our standard diet for rabbits and deer. She did not hesitate and soon tucked in with an appetite that disguised the fact that she was very ill.

Each day I walked to some nearby waste ground and picked bunches of fresh dandelion leaves, the absolute favourite of every rabbit. Each day I watched her, fearing that her nose would become inflamed, a symptom of the second stage of myxomatosis. I kept her eyes clean and noted how she was putting on weight with all that eating.

In the meantime I had scanned every book I possessed on animal diseases but not one even mentioned trying a cure. However, some did remark that there is natural resistance building up in wild populations and a few rabbits do recover spontaneously. Could Mikki be one of the lucky ones?

Our vet was reluctant to treat Mikki, but advised a course of antibiotics to fight any secondary infections (antibiotics would have no effect on the virus itself). We had now had her for eighteen days, and she must have had the disease for at least a week before I found her. That meant that she had been sick for twenty-five days, when the books all said that infected rabbits die at eighteen days into the disease. Now we really were beginning to hope.

Every day I picked dandelions for Mikki and bathed those eyes, but her nose started to swell and it seemed that the worst was happening: the disease was flaring up again. Then almost imperceptibly she began to move one of those swollen eyelids. They were so covered in necrotic skin that I really could not tell what was going on. Gritting my teeth I clamped onto the dead skin with forceps and started to pull it painfully away. The pink healthiness of new skin shone from underneath – her eyelids were healing. I carefully cleaned them up and applied a soothing ointment to the parts that were still obviously sore. Her eyes moved and the pink eyelids blinked more freely. With a few days' more treatment, she might be able to see again. She had now been with us for five weeks.

The swelling on her nose subsided but the new scar tissue around her eyes gradually formed a healthy pink curtain right over them until there was only a very small hole in each centre. She had probably healed a bit too well.

By this time a new vet, Ben Linnell from Tuckett, Gray and Partners, was attending to our severest cases. In our daily discussions I suggested some form of surgical intervention to Mikki's eyes. Without ruling this out, the vet suggested that we would need the assistance of a plastic surgeon experienced in the techniques of micro-surgery.

All our volunteer team had witnessed Mikki's battle for life and admired her super-rabbit efforts to overcome myxomatosis, and now they demanded daily bulletins on her health and recovery. I openly discussed the present problem and, lo and behold, it happened again: whenever one of our patients needs something

out of the ordinary it seems to appear, 'out of the blue' so to speak. This time a new member of our volunteer team, Clare Roberts, slipped in the bombshell that her husband, Jeremy, was an eminent plastic surgeon – she would ask him about Mikki's eyes.

Jeremy wasted no time in coming to the Hospital to assess the situation for himself. He was quite hopeful that the eyelids could be rebuilt, and he suggested that he should carry out the micro-surgical operation together with his colleague Mr Bruce Bailey.

My task was to co-ordinate the occasion, working with Ben Linnell, and Michelle Statham, the Trust's new veterinary nurse, in arranging the anaesthetic procedures. Rabbits are notoriously erratic under anaesthetic, and an added problem in this case was that there are

LEFT *Before the operation Mikki could only see slightly out of her left eye.*

BELOW *The two eminent plastic surgeons working on Mikki's eyes.*

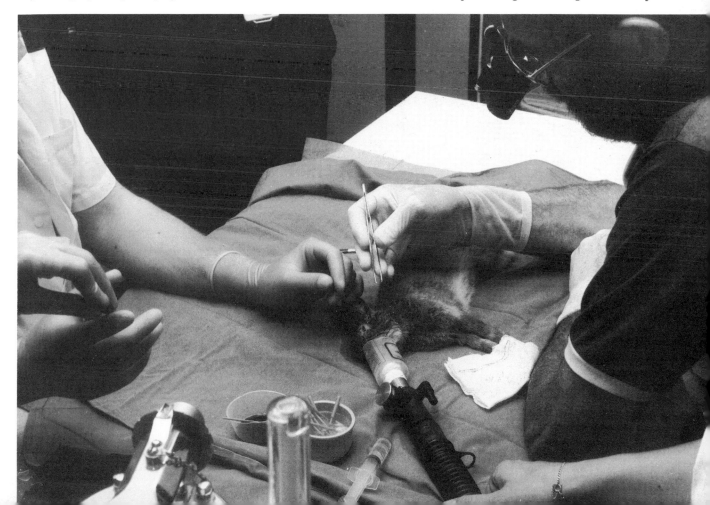

no specific face-masks to fit this kind of small mammal without interfering with the delicate surgical work on the eyes. After numerous trials and test fittings I finally concocted a mask from an empty Millpledge wound-powder bottle, with its bottom removed; this I attached to the anaesthetic machine through a similarly bottomless 5 millilitre syringe case, and the whole thing was held together with sticky plaster tape.

The following Wednesday evening found us all gathered at Tuckett and Gray's Veterinary Hospital, taking over their operating theatre. Mr Roberts and Mr Bailey were accompanied by one of their theatre sisters, Sister Celia Willis, who also handled all their specialised microsurgical equipment. Ben Linnell gave Mikki a pre-medication before fitting my 'Heath Robinson' anaesthetic mask (which, incidentally, worked a treat).

Mikki was soon sleeping peacefully but still the operation could not begin because we had no way of removing the fluffy hair growth that had sprouted on the new scar tissue. Normal veterinary and, for that matter, human shaving equipment is far too clumsy for this delicate operation but Mr Bailey had an answer: to use Immac, the proprietary hair remover used by women. Of course none of us had any to hand, but since it was 7.55 p.m. and Sainsbury's closed at eight I had just five minutes to sprint to the store. Ignoring my embarrassment, I managed to buy this feminine product.

At last the operation could proceed. Mikki gave us one more fright when she stopped breathing early on, but Michelle's intervention with artificial respiration soon had the rabbit breathing steadily and there were no more crises.

The two surgeons worked with finely tuned binocular-type eye-pieces fitted over their eyes. Swiftly and deftly they cut open the sealed eyelids and then with a minute curved needle sutured the outside skin to the conjunctival lining of each newly formed eyelid. I interrupted to ask about removing the stitches once the lids had healed but was told that they would be absorbed.

Mikki, fighter that she is, sailed through the operation and, after a few days' acclimatisation to the light that she hadn't seen for months, was as spritely as a spring lamb, jumping around her hospital cage and revelling in all those sights she must surely have missed. I am still putting ointment and drops in her eyes every hour throughout the day and every now and then have to borrow eyebrow tweezers to pluck a lash that interferes with her progress.

I am hoping to release her into Sally's farm, high in the Chilterns, but will wait for a month or two just to make sure that those eyelashes do not cause her too much trouble.

Les gives eye drops to Mikki after the operation.

7 Sticky Situations with Hedgehogs

The positive results from the Pieterburen seal hospital and our experiences with Mikki confirmed that viruses could be met head on and beaten. However, it also proved that to treat specialised species any experience is worth its weight in gold. Thanks to the many years that Lenie t'Hart has been looking after seals, it has been possible for us to include a small seal facility at the new Teaching Hospital and in a few years we should be able to include the care of seals on our training curriculum and in our educational publications.

In our own right we have, over the years, amassed vast experience of many species of animals. We originally intended to publish our findings once the new Hospital was operational, but the massacre of Britain's wildlife soon began to be so great that we felt an urgency to get going even before our desk-top publishing was operational.

Our book *The Complete Hedgehog* broke all the records in the sale of a one-animal specialist title. Its appearance on the *Sunday Times* bestseller list at No. 2 did a great deal to publicise the plight of the hedgehog and, at last, to provide factual helpful advice on how to help our prickly friends. Yet when we first started taking in hedgehogs nobody knew anything about their particular ups and downs.

It was true that most symptoms of disease and injury could be treated with veterinary drugs, but nobody knew dose rates for hedgehogs or whether they were allergic to some drugs, as dogs are to the ivermectin we use successfully on foxes, and as guinea pigs and rabbits are, I believe, to penicillin, which is the first line of attack on infections in many other animals.

We played it slowly and carefully, introducing new drugs only after tests had been carried out to prove their effectiveness. After many years and thousands of hedgehogs treated we felt confident enough to tell others of our findings and published a list of drugs and dosages for use with hedgehogs. As an addendum to *The Complete Hedgehog*, the drugs list has been snapped up by veterinarians and rehabilitators all over the country, and we know from our correspondence that it has saved many hedgehogs and will continue to do so.

Young hedgehogs with two rare albinos.

Every line in both *The Complete Hedgehog* and the drugs list was based on solid experience and we had the records to back them up. Naturally we generated a good deal of publicity, and as more people saw our work and knew our telephone number, the better it had to be for the cold, lonely, injured hedgehog – or any other animal, for that matter. We showed everybody not only how we were preserving the lives of hedgehogs but also that we knew, only too well, the elations and heartaches of caring for real animals and having to work extremely hard to keep the mucky little perishers clean.

The problems of skin diseases in hedgehogs is a case in point. Sounds rather grotty, doesn't it? But it's hell to a hedgehog to have a skin affliction with nobody doing anything about it. At the beginning there was a well-renowned veterinary manual that told us all how hedgehogs suffer greatly from ringworm but are not troubled with mange, caused by mites. Nothing could be further from the truth and over the years we have seen and treated quite a few hedgehogs with ringworm and hundreds with mites.

In New Zealand there were papers published on mites in hedgehogs, but there was nothing in this country where the problem is almost as rampant. We decided to publish our own findings but realised we could only put them all down on paper once we had a microscope and I could produce a photograph of the major mite

Hedgehog with a broken leg.

Caparinia tripilis. For a long while we were not even sure of the name of the mite because nobody else in this country had published either a photograph or drawing of the microscopic parasite.

However, we managed to buy a microscope with the great help of the manufacturers, Gillett and Sibert, and we were able to photograph the mite. The occasion of the British Wildlife Rehabilitation Council symposium was the forum at which we introduced a wonderfully explicit colour poster-paper on skin diseases in hedgehogs. This will now save a lot of hedgehogs from intense discomfort and often a slow lingering death.

Yet even with all this experience and material published there are still new problems that our thick little friends the hedgehogs are going to spring on us. A well-known hedgehog expert recently claimed in a radio interview that hedgehogs never break their backs. How I wish that were true! My constant great dread – and it's been realised on quite a few occasions – is that a hedgehog casualty will arrive with all the classic symptoms of having broken its back, usually in a road traffic accident.

On the few occasions that this has happened, I have always arranged an X-ray and in consultation with my vets, Tuckett, Gray and Partners, have then decided on a course of treatment or euthanasia.

The latest to be admitted was a large female hedgehog who had been hit by a car. She could only crawl around, pulling herself along with her front legs while her back legs dragged uselessly behind her.

One other symptom of a broken back is the failure of the bladder to express the body's fluid waste. The bladder is like a very fragile balloon constantly filling with fluid from the kidneys. If it is inoperative it soon swells and completely fills the abdomen cavity and worst of all encourages infection, often in the form of cystitis. Manually expressing a hedgehog's paralysed bladder can mean the difference between life and death.

Milly, as I named this hedgehog, was already in trouble with her bladder. As I felt for it and applied gentle pressure I knew that one slight slip and I could burst her bladder, causing peritonitis, which at present is invariably fatal in hedgehogs. Very carefully I squeezed, dreading the sudden deflation that would mean I had burst it. Nothing happened. For once I did not manage to express any fluid whatsoever.

Later in the day I had arranged for Milly to have an X-ray to assess the damage to her spine, and I thought that, rather than subject her to more manhandling now, I would try again then.

The X-ray did not show any damage to the spine, and so we could only assume that her paralysis was neurologically induced and would perhaps get better in time. In fact even in the short time she had been with us we could notice a slight recovery in movement in her left hind leg.

But overnight Milly started to chew her right hind leg. Sometimes this is a good sign that feeling, or pins and needles, are returning to a limb but the chewing has to be stopped before the damage becomes too extensive. By coincidence at that time, I had just been given some samples by Leo Laboratories, and one of them was a bitter spray which prevented this kind of self-mutilation, a not uncommon occurrence in many small animals.

For a whole week I sprayed the foot and suffered the nerve-wracking trauma of massaging her bloated bladder still with very poor results. On the eighth day I was once more standing over the sink, Milly sprawled across my hands, making the kind of encouraging noises you might make to a baby being potty-trained. All of a sudden I noticed a large hard swelling and then the little pink nose and two feet of a baby hedgehog appeared for a moment and disappeared again. Quickly I panicked, and I put her back in her warm cage. Had I forced a baby out of her womb by squeezing too hard? Had I forced her to abort?

I didn't know. I had never dealt with small animal obstetrics before. But surely this situation could occur with cats and small dogs? I had to phone the vets! They might have some suggestions for how I could retrieve the situation.

The vets were not at all worried. There was no way I could have caused an abortion with

Les with Milly, the car accident victim.

A–Z of Garden Hazards for Hedgehogs

Barbed wire   Keep all barbed wire at least a foot above the ground, and never leave it trailing or discarded on the ground. If a hedgehog manages to become impaled on a spike it will curl into a ball and become hopelessly enmeshed.

Bonfires   Piles of dry leaves, rolled up newspapers, twigs and wood are irresistible to hedgehogs looking for a nest or some shelter. So always check bonfires by carefully turning them over before you set them alight.

Compost Heaps   These are ideal nest sites for hedgehogs which are often injured when the compost is forked or turned. Break the heap down carefully, and if you find a nest of hedgehogs leave them alone. They will move of their own accord eventually.

Drains   Uncovered drains are a common cause of distress, especially the small waste traps outside many kitchens. So cover all drains, and if you find a hedgehog well and trully trapped in a drain pull it out by clamping two pairs of pliers onto its spines and lifting it gently.

Fungicides   (*See* Wood Preserver)

Garages   If there is a pit, or a tray of old sump oil left lying around, a hedgehog is likely to fall into it. They are also likely to investigate open tins of paint or other liquids, so always replace the lids. If a hedgehog does get covered in oil, wash it in a hand-hot 2 per cent solution of washing-up liquid. Rinse it thoroughly in warm water and keep it indoors and warm for at least a day. Paint and tar can be removed with Swarfega, but make sure it is washed off well. (*See also* Sheds)

Herbicides   (*See* Pesticides and Weedkiller)

Insect Killers   (*See* Pesticides and Slug Pellets)

Lawn Mowers   Sometimes hedgehogs will snuggle down unnoticed in tall grass and can be caught with blades and strimmers. So walk the area to be mowed to check for small animals and nests.

Netting   This can become a snare as twine gets caught around the hedgehog's spines. As it struggles to escape the strands form ligatures which can tourniquet limbs.

Keep all netting or string arrangements a foot from the ground, and never leave them lying around in the garden.

Oil   (*See* Garages)

Paint   (*See* Garages)

Pesticides   Many of these contain deadly poisons, so try not to use them. Organic methods are just as effective and safer too. Soapy water is good for spraying on aphids and other insects, and there is a wide selection of safer insect killers on the market. Read the packets carefully and always mix according to the instructions.

Pets   Apart from badgers, dogs are the only other animals that regularly injure hedgehogs. Keep your dog under control at all times, and if your dog discovers something worth barking at in the garden

find out what it is. Both the hedgehog and the dog are likely to get hurt in a conflict.

Ponds Hedgehogs swim very well, but if they cannot escape from a pool they will become exhausted and drown. By laying a ramp or by gently sloping the banks of your pond you'll ensure that hedgehogs can escape. (*See also* Swimming Pools)

Rubbish Hedgehogs are frequently killed in various forms by rubbish, so always ensure that your garden is clear of it. Cover dustbins and tie up refuse sacks so the contents can't blow away.

Broken glass and other sharp objects are obviously a hazard and can be a danger to humans too.

Hedgehogs often get their heads stuck in things and end up starving to death. Empty tin cans, yoghurt pots and other cartons which once contained food are a common cause of injury, distress and death, because hedgehogs cannot resist trying to finish off what remains inside them. Empty tin cans with the lids still attached can decapitate a hedgehog.

Ring-pulls from cans, and the plastic rings that bind six-packs of canned drinks are also major hazards to hedgehogs. Babies especially can simply walk into the rings. At first there is no problem, but as the baby grows the ring tightens around its body. Many hedgehogs die a slow painful death in this way.

Sheds Hedgehogs regularly nest under sheds and outbuildings and are often injured when the shed is demolished or moved. So always check for hedgehogs by lifting the floor carefully. If a nest is there with youngsters DO NOT DISTURB THEM but postpone the work for about a month.

Slug Pellets Never use slug pellets. The poison they contain almost always kills hedgehogs who like the pellets every bit as much as the slugs do. Hedgehogs are also killed because they eat the poisoned slugs. Alternative methods of slug control are effective. Scatter rose twigs or nettles around the plants you want to protect, or sink a cup of old beer into the ground – this attracts and then drowns slugs. There is also a safe slug killer on the market called Fertosan.

String (*See* Netting)

Swimming Pools Leave a flat piece of wood about a foot square floating in the swimming pool. If a hedgehog falls in, it can swim to the 'raft' where it can wait for rescue. Check the pool raft each day. (*See also* Ponds)

Tar (*See* Garages)

Weedkiller (*See* Pesticides)

Wood Preserver Many wood preservers are poisonous and will harm hedgehogs as they frequently lick freshly treated fences. Ask for an environmentally safe water-based product at your garden centre. (*See also* Pesticides and Slug Pellets)

pressure on the bladder; the hedgehog baby had probably died when Milly was injured and now could be causing a severe obstruction. It had to be removed.

Being a hedgehog midwife was a new experience for me and one I faced with great trepidation. I anaesthetised Milly in my hedgehog unrolling machine, to save her any discomfort, and applied liberal amounts of lubricant to aid the passage of any obstruction. Gently I squeezed her bladder. The tiny swelling appeared, followed by the tiny pink nose and feet. Telling myself over and over again that the baby was already dead, I grasped the nose with small forceps and gently pulled. It would not budge, and yet the vets said that it had to come out. I applied more pressure and slowly the rest of the baby appeared. It had been severely injured in the accident and could never have been born without my intervention – and it had clearly been causing a blockage.

Milly still has not recovered the use of her right leg and her bladder but she eats and drinks as though there were nothing wrong with her. It's going to be some time before she is fully recovered, but she has done nothing but improve since my intervention and introduction to hedgehog obstetrics.

I think that hedgehog road casualties are in the main unavoidable, with neither the hedgehog nor the driver capable of changing the situation. I would not go as far as to say that hedgehogs are stupid to cross carriageways; but in many other situations hedgehogs do amply express the primitive nature of their brains – which more succinctly means that they are a little bit slow-witted. Leave a hazard around and a hedgehog will blunder into it. This year alone I have had either to rescue or bury dozens of hedgehogs that had: got themselves stuck in gaps in walls; become tangled in bean netting, cricket netting and tennis netting; and fallen into pits, drains, swimming pools, ponds, bowls of oil, tins of paint and even a motor car engine. One particular casualty who really did rack my innovative powers was brought to the Hospital one very warm June evening when I was out conducting our tree-planting group around the new site for St Tiggywinkles at Watermead, on the northern fringes of Aylesbury.

I had parked the car with the roof open and luckily had more or less finished one circuit of the area when my car phone rang across the open space letting me know that I was wanted back at the Hospital. I tried to converse with Sue, back at base, but as always my car phone cut us off in mid-sentence. However, I had managed to pick up that a gosling with fishing line hanging from its mouth and a hedgehog covered in what sounded like glue had both arrived at the Hospital and needed my immediate attention.

I went straight back, leaving the tree-planting group having tea around Dennis Furnell's caravanette. The glue had already set on the hedgehog and so I first went into action to try to remove the line, and hook, from the oesophagus of the gosling.

My technique, which has proved successful, even in the field, on ducks, geese and swans, requires a reel of cotton, a length of narrow plastic tube and some form of palatable lubricant such as liquid paraffin. The cotton is securely tied to the end of the fishing line protruding from the beak. (A pair of artery forceps clamped on the fishing line will prevent it disappearing down the bird's throat.) The cotton is fed through the plastic tube, and the tube, plastered in lubricant, is then slid over the cotton, over the fishing line and into the bird's throat. It is slowly fed farther down the neck until finally it stops at the hook. A very gentle push dislodges the hook which will then sit in the mouth of the tube. Very, very carefully the tube, line and hook are slid back out of the throat, with pauses if the hook snags onto anything. Simply yanking the tube out could cause damage to the delicate walls of the oesophagus.

As it happened, the very fine line was also wound around the base of the gosling's tongue, causing some necrosis, and this needed the intervention of an anaesthetic and a vet.

I could now concentrate on 'Sticky', the hedgehog firmly stuck in a half-rolled position to the newspaper at the bottom of his cardboard box. As I tore him off, the extent of the thick blanket of glue covering his underside and some of his spines made me wonder what I ought to do. The man who had brought the hedgehog said that he had tried to cut the glue off but had only added to Sticky's problems by slicing into his skin. He had brought with him a tin of

HOOKED BIRD EMERGENCY KIT

60 cm plastic tube 7 mm O.D. (available from motor spares shop)
Reel of sewing thread
Bottle of oral lubricant (liquid paraffin)
Small scissors
Pair of wire cutters
Wound powder (Sulphacrin by Millpledge)
Pair of artery forceps
Pair of needle-nosed pliers

If you can reach the hook, the barb at the end will prevent your being able to remove it easily – so first cut off the 'eye' and then push the hook through, carefully, barbed end first.

solvent which he assured us would remove the glue but warned that it was reputed to cause skin cancer. We could not take the chance, either for the hedgehog or for us.

Once more a wildlife casualty required innovation and improvisation. Trying to unroll Sticky was impossible as the glue, which was some form of carpet adhesive, had him stuck fast in that half-rolled position. Taking my curved-bladed scissors I started to cut away the spines covered in glue. Fortunately the glue had not penetrated to the base of the spines and so I was able to cut a clear area, albeit now devoid of spines. However, under his legs and body I did not dare snip away with scissors for fear of cutting into his many folds of soft skin. I gently but firmly tugged at a piece of the glue. It came away, but then so did a small clump of fur, causing Sticky to flinch. This was obviously the way to remove the glue but it was also a way of torturing a hedgehog. I would have to anaesthetise him. As he slept, it was only me that flinched as I teased and tugged all his fur off, as gently as I could. Within five minutes he was a clean though temporarily bald hedgehog. Within a few hours he would forget the discomfort, and he would soon grow more hair, but unfortunately he was unlikely to have learnt his lesson and when released he could easily repeat the whole sticky episode.

It took me some time to clean up the surgery and myself after that little incident, and just as I finished a midnight call came through from Beaconsfield: a female muntjac deer was firmly wedged in a wrought iron gate. It's amazing how incidents like this, that are the real nitty-gritty of our rescue work at St Tiggywinkles, can never be planned for. When we were making our video film of the work of the Hospi-

Les untangles the female muntjac wedged in a wrought iron gate.

tal we only had one rescue in the whole 4 days it took to film it. And that was of a very ungrateful heron trapped in fishing line. When you pick up a heron it's somewhat of a wrestling match, with a lethal beak, two enormous wings and a pair of gangly legs all to be controlled and folded into a carrying box — a very ungainly rescue. To rescue a muntjac doe is a much more orderly affair. I went out to this deer and soon freed her from the gate.

The video film we were making was to show, in fifteen minutes, how our Wildlife Hospital Trust has become the leader in the care of wild animals and birds in this country. Geared to our appeal for the new St Tiggywinkles teaching hospital it would detail our plans for the future and, we hoped, encourage potential donors to pledge financial support for the new buildings. The cost of making videos is astronomical but our perennial supporters, the British Petroleum Company plc, came forward to cover the production costs.

There are, of course, costs over and above those of production, for instance for the scriptwriter, the director and the actors. Once again the ethereal power that seems always to manifest itself when the animals need help came to our rescue. The champion of birdwatching, Bill Oddie, insisted on preparing a script and then putting his experience from in front of the camera behind the camera, as producer. We all remember the Goodies television scenes with their sophisticated techniques and original production. Next Bill called on an old Goodies chum, Graeme Garden, who without hesitation agreed to pull the film together as director. This was quite a sacrifice on Graeme's part as he spends a great deal of his working life directing training videos for the prestigious Video Arts Company. And not only did he give of his valuable expertise but, with Bill, he also persuaded Video Arts to make the film, keeping costs to a minimum. Wincey Willis and Colin Baker, and Bill as well, would appear in cameo roles, while John Craven would do the narration. With this backing, *Who Cares?* just had to be a success.

We filmed in August which gave us a good chance of some decent weather. Once again we were smiled upon, with four days of clear blue skies. To start the filming we shot many seemingly unrelated pieces around the Hospital and in the intensive care unit. Luckily I had to work with some patients, in particular a seriously injured hedgehog which came in during the first day. I might have been short of experience in speaking to a camera, but when I have an animal in front of me there is no shutting me up.

The filming went well, especially a sequence showing a coot release, when the bird splashed its way across the surface of the lake straight towards the camera. We did acquire some interested bystanders: a woman, her child and their very wet dripping dog who had been for a swim in the lake. Before long this woman's ribald comments started to affect the sound recording.

Many video sequences were shot at the Hospital.

'What's that?' she demanded, pointing at the microphone in its hairy cover (a Dougal to the trade).

'Are yer filming?'

'Is it going on the telly?'

None of our crew responded, not even when her dog sprayed them all after another dip in the lake.

We moved off. She followed. We stopped. She stopped. All the time she was cackling her inane remarks.

Finally, as she seemed about to leave, she came over to us and pointed at Bill.

'I know you, don't I?'

This was not surprising as Bill is one of the best known faces on television. We waited for the 'I've seen you on the telly'.

But no, she had made her mind up.

'You're one of my dustmen. Ain't yer?'

We all rolled up. Bill, for once, was lost for a quick reply, but fortunately at that moment her dog ran off and she tore after it, cursing.

The children featured so stunningly in the video were models of good manners and behaviour. Mind you, that old adage of working with children and animals came doubly true for three of the Trust's Vice-Presidents who it seems had thrown all caution to the wind in order to make our video a success.

The first to suffer was Colin Baker who, in the film, was to take a party of children around the Hospital, talking generally about the animals and asking the occasional question. One particular fox, a road traffic casualty recovering from a broken leg, had the habit – peculiar in a fox – of sitting outside during the day, completely spurning his nice, dark, secure sleeping quarters. On camera, Colin led his party of children to the fox's pen and launched into questions and answers about foxes. Towards the end of the fox session, he asked the children for a name for the fox. As quick as a flash young Robert responded with, 'Let's call him Squasho. After all, he was run over by a car.'

On a re-run of the video you could see Colin explode into laughter, and, judging by the sea-sick motion of the camera, so did Mike Spragg, the cameraman – another out-take fit for Denis Norden's *It'll Be All Right on the Night*.

Wincey Willis, meanwhile, had been standing in the wings cuddling Baldrick. Baldrick is

ABOVE *Bill Oddie and the camera crew with some of the children featured in the video.*

BELOW *Wincey Willis and Graeme Garden waiting in the wings.*

ABOVE *Colin Baker watching the proceedings with interest.*   BELOW *Wincey takes her group of children around the aviaries.*

far from being the prettiest dog ever, but some-how his little watering eyes capture every heart and for a cuddle he will stay quiet all day. He has his funny ways that none of us understands: he will not sit on anybody's lap but will stand or else sit to the side of them. Oh, the stories he could horrify us with if he could talk.

Wincey had her group of children to conduct around the aviaries. Being very knowledgeable about birds and, for once, being very serious, she could really get her group involved in depth in the subject. However, even Wincey met her match in front of the kestrel aviary. Fully aware that social conditions could affect children's at-titudes to wildlife, she asked if any of her group had seen the film *Kes*. Expecting a yes or no she got the instant reply, 'No, but have you seen the new James Bond film?'

Another out-take for the cutting room floor.

Even the animals got in on the act. We had a badger to release on the other side of Watford where Andy Walton and I had picked her up three days before. She had been hit by a car and had then fled through a hedgerow into a large field. It took Andy and me three-quarters of an hour to reach the area, where we realised at once that we had a lengthy search on our hands . . . but that was not all. In the dark as I climbed over the gate into the field I was met with a violent fiery snorting. I nearly fell off the gate but Andy, behind me with the large spotlight, shone a beam onto the dragon – two enormous, beautiful horses obviously madly interested in what we were doing. I have never handled a horse, let alone two giants like these, but as the people who had seen the badger were watching I had to appear to be unmoved and walk between the steaming snorts. I suggested that Andy did the same, but no, he actually went up to the horses, slapped them on the neck and literally pushed them away.

'I didn't know you knew anything about horses,' I spluttered quizzically, but immensely relieved.

'Oh! When I was a lad I used to help with the pony rides on the Majorca beaches.'

Another side of the versatile Andy of which I had known nothing.

To cut a long story short, we found the badger in a barn, took her back to the Hospital for observation, and were now ready, three days later, to let her go back to her home.

The stage was set: Graeme had his camera running, Andy had the badger in her basket ready, as soon as it was opened, to head out across the field, giving plenty of footage for the cameraman. I gave a splendid example of how not to handle those giant horses but managed to lead them out of the arena. Cameras rolling. At the count of three Andy opened the basket. The badger hesitated, sniffed the cold evening air, leapt from the basket, ran 5 metres straight at the camera and then disappeared from view into a small copse which she obviously knew quite well. On the re-run we had about five seconds of badger release, but at least enough to show that we do get our casualties back to the wild.

Andy Walton releases the badger.

The little owl releases were even more comical, with one of them threatening to dive into the stream which ran past the release site. Sue was carrying out these releases, and her own display – sliding down a steep bank on her bottom – was captured on camera forever by Wincey at the top of the bank.

On that day we also filmed the release of a grass snake and the somersaulting leap for freedom of a weasel, showing that all wild creatures are equally important in the field of wildlife rescue.

Through all these ups and downs, hilarious moments and the serious care of newly-arrived casualties, Graeme somehow managed to tie the film together. John Craven provided the superbly presented link commentary so that after four days it was 'a wrap'.

At the end of it all Graeme had produced sixteen minutes of video film worthy, in my opinion, of an animal Oscar. Video Arts converted a copy to 16 millimetre film for showing on the large screen at our official Appeal launch later in the year.

All the paperwork of the regenerated appeal was to be dealt with at Pemberton Close – a daunting prospect because we already did not have enough room to swing a cat, hypothetically speaking. Our dining room, which served as an office, was crammed full to the gunwales, and as we were taking on our first full-time office staff worker, young Clare Johnson, who had served the Trust as a diligent volunteer for many years, we really had to make some other arrangement. We did not really want to spend money on building an extension to the house and so we plumped for a fully kitted-out portable building – a Portakabin.

Over the years we have always kept a low

RIGHT *The grass snake is as important as the next animal when it comes to wildlife rescue.*

It is hard to keep a low profile when a 90-foot crane delivers a Portakabin.

profile locally. In fact many visitors, on seeing the outside fence and garden thought they had the wrong house. Most are amazed at the Tardis effect of cramming so much into a ridiculously small space. However, on the day the office arrived, the whole world knew what was going on. To start with we had a 30-metre crane parked in the road, and then the Portakabin was dumped unceremoniously on the grass verge. I am glad the crane driver knew what he was doing as he lifted the office right over the top of the house into the back garden. The precision was amazing as he gently lowered it into position, just 15 centimetres from the small bird aviary and 30 centimetres from the dining room window. Good old Nigel Brock found somebody to wire the building into the mains and the new appeal office was operational.

In September 1988 we were to publicly launch the appeal. Our good friends the British Petroleum Company plc offered to host the launch at their prestigious headquarters in the City of London. There was a cinema where we could show, for the first time, the completed film *Who Cares?*, a leading part of our appeal strategy. We were advised that to get two hundred people to attend the launch we would need to send out a thousand invitations to large companies and grant-making trusts. I have always believed that 'somebody up there' looks after the needs of animals, but he chose September 1988 to go on holiday and let the Post Office go on strike. We could not even get out our invitations, let alone expect replies.

Les and Sue with Wincey Willis and Bill Oddie at the appeal launch.

I say we were left on our own but we weren't really, for at that time Wincey was given a Rank-Xerox fax machine and she let us use it to get our invitations out. It was still very hard work, with Sue and Clare working flat out to telephone everybody on the voluminous lists that I kept producing, but it worked, and the launch was saved: it was a great day with plenty of buzz and the appeal proper was underway.

After the launch Colin, our son, took over the fundraising baton and before long the dream of the Teaching Hospital had financial supporters. It would be impractical to list all the donors so far, there will be a Roll of Honour in a promi-nent position in the building. It is enough to say that, following British Petroleum's lead, British Telecom is providing the administration block, the London Brick Company the bricks, and Crabtree the electrical fittings, and the Centre is starting to take shape.

It is good to have Colin working for the Trust. He has lived with it for eleven years and, to his credit, he did not ask for a position as soon as he left school but instead went out into the cut-throat world of marketing for a few years, to learn his trade. Whereas I am confident of my ability with animals and figures, I bow to Colin as master in his own field.

8 Away from It All

With Colin working full time for the Trust there was an added benefit for Sue and me, which was worth more than all the money one can imagine. Colin could stand in for us, not only during the day but also overnight. He could be available to see in the casualties and generally take responsibility for running the place while we, for the first time in twelve years, could manage a short break with no ties.

We did not immediately take the opportunity to go away but in the end circumstances demanded it: we both became the unwilling victims of what the Americans diagnose as 'burn out'.

It all came to a head after a routine 'wild goose chase' for a deer. The deer, a large fallow doe, had been hit by a car on the outskirts of Ashridge Forest just beyond Tring railway station. She had apparently managed to struggle off the road and was now recumbent in the corner of an empty field. Andy was still at work – it was late afternoon – and so I called him and arranged to rendezvous at the field which was comparatively near his place of work. The caller who had notified us agreed to

go back to the scene and help us with the deer. Everything looked set for an easy rescue.

However, the best laid plans of mice and men don't allow for the amazing resilience and ingenuity of wild animals. When we arrived there was no sign of the deer. The early evening was dark and frosty, especially along the forest edge where the trees which rose above the field were the domain of a tawny owl calling eerily to its mate. The deer, which we were assured could not walk, seemed to have managed to get into the forest and was probably lying up, suffering, somewhere in the depths. There was nothing for it but to start a bush-to-bush search in the hope of finding her still alive.

For two hours the three of us climbed laboriously up into the forest, spreading out to cover as much territory as possible. Every few minutes we would stop and listen just in case she was trying to move through the brittle undergrowth. There was nothing other than the hidden tawny owl circling our progress. For searching at night we use high-powered rechargeable lamps which work beautifully for two hours and then quickly fade to a dim glow.

Our lamps had run down so it was in pitch black that we stumbled our tortuous way back to the car.

When you are searching for an injured animal you never want to give up but it is possible to search fruitlessly for hour after hour, especially for deer which, if they are even slightly mobile, can travel right out of the area in the few minutes that it takes you to get to the scene. On this occasion, with no more portable light, we decided to have one more try using the four-wheel drive Toyota Tercel with its free-running quartz-halogen spotlight. Andy sat on top of the car directing the spotlight into the undergrowth while I drove slowly around the perimeter of the field. We found nothing. By now the frost was forming a white blanket over the ground. It was this frost that at last unravelled the mystery of the missing deer for, as we came to the end of our circumnavigaton, there outlined in the hoar were the tracks of a motor vehicle that had plainly driven up to our recumbent deer, reversed out with it, and driven off in the time it had taken us to arrive on the scene. To many people a motionless deer is simply various venison joints on the hoof, horrible though it may sound.

I would hate to tell you how many times we have been called out to injured fallow deer, only to find they have been carted off to a local butcher, who 'has an arrangement' in such situations. However, I would like to give a word of caution to all venison eaters. Deer meat does not go through the rigorous meat inspection processes that other animals do. Consequently the unseen horrors in a joint of venison can make Edwina Currie's salmonella-in-eggs scare look like a children's tea party.

At the time, the fruitless search did not seem all that strenuous, but the hectic year must have been catching up on me because the following morning I was totally exhausted. In fact I slept solidly for two days while everyone else ran the Hospital. Something must have been wrong because I am normally the last one to flag and would think nothing of being up night after night on animal calls. The following day I actually managed to beat the local doctor's appointment system and receptionist.

I think that really I knew the diagnosis even before I breached the defences at the surgery. I was a victim of 'burn out' – I had been burning my candle at both ends and in the middle. The doctor's prescription for a cure was a few days 'away from it all'. The Hospital does not govern my life but two weeks later Sue and I found a lull in cases and appointments, enough to contemplate a few days by the sea.

My first thoughts were of a busman's holiday in Norfolk where, in between eating, sleeping and more eating, we could call in on the Docking set-up to see how the seals were faring. We could also visit our friends Len and Sheila Baker who run Swan Rescue (Europe) and put in as many hours with injured birds as we do.

Les rescues a fallow buck – the victim of a Deer Traffic Accident.

They are certainly no strangers to 'burn out'.

Len and Sheila have worked up and down the country for many years, like us, living with the horrors which are inflicted on wildlife both accidentally and intentionally in man's world. Len is a most wonderful character. Always in his flying suit working togs he invariably has a story to tell. Sometimes his stories are a bit colourful but I could listen to him for hours and with Sheila's renowned hospitality a visit would be a must – that is, unless they were off somewhere around Britain rescuing swans.

They would go to the ends of the earth to help a swan and it was Len whom I phoned when I heard on my car radio one night as I was going out on a badger call, that the RSPCA Inspector at Berwick-on-Tweed was shooting a flock of swans which had become embroiled in an oil spill on the river. In an instant Len was on his way and, with the help of the RSPCA Head Office who until my call knew nothing of the incident, stopped the killing and managed to clean and release all the surviving swans.

In my opinion it was Len's campaigning on behalf of his local swans on the Norfolk Broads that forced the Government to ban the sale of lead fishing weights. Effective to a degree, the legislation was as always watered down when the Government left it up to local water authorities to ban the use of weights. For this reason

ABOVE *Les catching an extremely smelly swan.*

Les and Andy Walton bathing Pongie.

there are still many anglers irresponsibly using lead weights and of course swans suffering the long, lingering, wasting death of lead poisoning.

However, Len now has a new method of curing the poisoning, but in true Len fashion he surrounds his system with mystery and flamboyancy. All he will tell us is that the system involves the use of a secondhand aircraft engine. Our minds boggle and we smile a little, and so does he.

His knowledge of swans and swan ailments is phenomenal and I know that if I have a swan query Len will willingly give me an answer plus a few more anecdotes. It's a tonic for me to phone him.

We quite regularly take swans into our Hospital. In fact they are one of the four species, along with deer, badgers and foxes, that we regard as 'heavy rescue' and launch a rescue team to bring in. On many occasions it's just swans being silly and crash-landing in high streets and people's gardens. Occasionally, especially when they are trailing angler's line and float, they are on the water, necessitating the launch of *Rescuer One*, our inflatable rescue boat.

Last week I was reminded of one idiot swan that I had to go out and rescue at Rickmansworth. The local branch of the Caravan Club invited Sue and me along to their winter meeting to collect a cheque for a tremendous £850 that the younger members had collected towards our appeal. The high point of the evening turned out to be the great laughter at my expense when one of the caravanners reminded me that he worked at the sewage farm where I had had to catch an exceedingly smelly swan.

It had crash-landed not on a roadway but in an open tank, as big as a tennis court, of untreated sewage. The swan smelt, the tank smelt, everything smelt absolutely awful. It wasn't the swan's size which worried me but the state he was in, covered in goodness knows what. Taking my life in my hands I grabbed him and unceremoniously stuffed him into one of the special swan-bags I had had made by a sailmaker in the Isle of Wight. At least we could hose that out afterwards, but what about me and the car? We all now smelled just like the swan.

I shot back to Aylesbury with all the windows wide open, and took him in the back way – if I had gone through the house as normal I am sure Sue would have been very displeased. Quickly I turned on the hosepipe and showered him. The gunge would not shift and so I was forced to bath him in washing-up liquid and hot water until he was clean, although by then I smelt even worse. Then it was my turn. All my clothes were off and into the Hospital washing machine while I bathed in almost pure Dettol. People think of swans as pristine white paragons but believe me they can be the muckiest of all our patients. I do not envy Len his garden full of them.

This swan was christened Pongie, although for a time I was just as suited to the nickname. Thankfully he was not injured through his crazy landing and we planned to release him a few days later onto a nice clean reservoir. However, he had the last laugh. When a swan flies you can hear the whistle of those powerful wings and two days later from inside the house I heard the unmistakable whistle of a swan flying by the window. Pongie had released himself. I only hope that nobody was walking past the garden fence as this Jumbo of a bird did a low level pass before disappearing over nearby houses and into the distance. I never saw or smelled him again.

On thinking about all the traumas we have endured with swans and the hectic life at Swan Rescue, it seemed that perhaps Norfolk was not such a good idea. Perhaps we should consider returning to Guernsey?

Earlier in the year we had flown to Guernsey to present a talk to the Ladies' Luncheon Club, at the prestigious St Pierre Park Hotel. We had stayed there for an extra few days to have some time off, hiring a car in which to see more of the island.

It does not matter where we go: there always seem to be animals to treat. In Guernsey it was not too long before I was tracked down to look at an injured hedgehog. Its back legs were hanging uselessly, just like Milly's – it showed all the symptoms of a broken back. Audrie Dickens, who looked after us so well in Guernsey, arranged for me to get an X-ray at a local vet's. My worst fear was confirmed; there was nothing anybody could do to save that hedgehog.

The other animal which needed our help was the duck we rescued from the main road outside the Co-op in St Peter Port. It was not yet injured so we could safely release it on a private waterway to which Audrie took us. On the last day of our trip we arranged to go to Jersey to call on Mr John Walker Bow, an ardent animal lover whose garden was amazing, with wild rabbits and thousands of birds coming to the hand to be fed. It was Mr Bow who arranged for a disabled herring gull named Bella to be flown to Heathrow by British Airways so that we could take over her care.

Almost a working trip, the week in Guernsey and Jersey had been superb, but now the flying which I hate seemed too much of a challenge so we crossed them both off our list and decided to be less ambitious: we would go down to the South Coast, to Brighton. In order to get completely away from it all I even left the car in Aylesbury and we travelled down by train. Having been spoilt at the St Pierre Park Hotel in Guernsey we wanted a good hotel. I telephoned the Brighton Information Centre who told us of a new luxury hotel just opened overlooking the sea.

We should have spotted at once that it was not our kind of hotel for though the room was superb, overlooking the winter sea and with all mod cons, there was something critical missing – a teapot and tea-making facilities. This was a disaster, as I live on cups of tea. Room service was the answer, and two cups of tea were delivered by a maid in a smart tailored suit. This was great but it put £3 on the bill. Still, I didn't mind as long as Sue was happy and we were getting a break.

The time for dinner arrived and we presented ourselves at the restaurant. The menu looked good if a bit pricey, and they had that wonderful fish, brill, which we had so enjoyed on Guernsey. It came – a mere pimple of fish in the centre of a large dish with about half a dozen vegetables. After the snack Sue and I trudged the night streets of Brighton searching for a Wimpy. We checked out the next day.

In nearby Eastbourne I knew a kindred spirit in Margaret King who runs a bird hospital. I phoned her and asked about hotels in Eastbourne. She told us of a small family hotel, not the Ritz but very comfortable. Sue and I were by now out for adventure so we decided to take the bus: along the coast, over Beachy Head (not literally), and into Eastbourne. We had not been on a bus for years but somehow managed the intricacies of paying the fare. It was great. Now we were really on holiday.

The hotel was a pleasant surprise: there was tea on tap, and in the little garden outside our window numerous bird feeders were under attack from flocks of blue tits – good research material for my next book, *The Complete Garden Bird*.

Once settled in we walked to see Margaret at her bird hospital. Margaret is an indomitable woman who has devoted her life to the care of injured birds, even after a bout of the serious chest complaint 'bird fancier's lung'. I often

Bella recovers after her aeroplane flight from Jersey.

think that it would be great if, say, a local builder would allow one or two of his men to spend a week every few months to help women like Margaret, doing all the heavy jobs around the place. Margaret, of course, was very busy with plenty of gulls and other seabirds, and had a room chock full of the grist of a bird hospital: blackbirds, thrushes, collared doves and sparrows.

We had two or three days to explore and spent many hours walking along the deserted beaches. We laughed at a novice wind surfer enduring fall after fall into the icy water. And we were saddened to come across a dead guillemot that had perished for no obvious reason. I began to wonder how things were going back in Aylesbury.

If you live on adrenaline, as we have done for years, when you slow down it seems that all the bugs you have kept at bay finally get through your defences. I had started to cough when we arrived in Eastbourne and over the next two days this developed into full-blown flu with all its depressing symptoms. I said to Sue, 'I might just as well be miserable at home.' She agreed, so we packed up and took the train back to Aylesbury, where I could wallow in self-pity in my own bed.

9 Back to Badgers

Inevitably, even with the flu, I came back to a hedgehog emergency. It was quite late in the year, a time always difficult for late broods of hedgehogs who often get caught by early frosts. Ernie, as he became known, was an orphan. Only a few days old, he was already undernourished and in trouble. To add to these familiar problems there was an enormous swelling all down one side of his tummy. This suggested a hernia, where the muscle wall over the abdomen is ruptured allowing the intestines to protrude; with such a condition there is the imminent likelihood of a fatal constriction. We more usually meet this kind of injury in larger hedgehogs, often as the result of a road traffic accident, and on one horrific occasion when some louts used the hedgehog as a football – once again, due to our inept wildlife laws, nothing could be done in this case to prosecute the villains.

There was no way of knowing what had caused Ernie's problem but we did know that the vet would have to operate without delay. I laid Ernie out on the seemingly enormous operating table, and he looked smaller than ever,

A makeshift anaesthetic mask was used for Ernie's operation.

lost among the drapes and swabs. There wasn't an anaesthetic mask small enough for him. In fact, we could have got all of him into the smallest. We had to improvise again and fashioned a makeshift mask out of a plastic syringe cover. I held his head in the 'mask' until he was asleep and then cleaned up the site where the incision would be made. So tiny was Ernie that every time the vet touched him he slid across the table. I had to slip my hand under the drapes, making sure not to touch any of the sterile operation site, and hold him with two fingers throughout the whole operation.

It took about thirty minutes to complete the finicky operation and, because Ernie was too young to have any hair we had to keep him warm afterwards as he woke up. Hedgehogs do grow a fine covering of hair on their underneaths but this does not come through until the hedgehog is about two weeks old.

He was still being bottle fed and, although the hernia site was secure, we found ourselves being over-cautious and quite clumsy as we tried to avoid his enormous stitches during the feeding and toileting process. Ten days later his stitches were out, hair was growing over the wound site, and he was developing into a normal young hedgehog wallowing in his food at the same time as eating it.

I think that, because we have broken the ground, more and more veterinary surgeons around the country are willing to have a go with new surgical techniques to save wildlife. I have heard of both a hysterectomy and an intravenous drip being used in hedgehog treatment. All day we are taking phone calls from vets about obscure hedgehog cases.

The only pity is that there is still a lot of misguided prejudice not only about hedgehogs but also about some of our most stunning wild mammals and birds. Often because of old, and new, propaganda from gamekeepers, many species are still tarred, feathered and gibbeted under the misnomer of vermin.

I will never forget how one of our most compassionate woman volunteers reacted to a young weasel I was hand-rearing.

'Oh!' she exclaimed. 'Now they *are* vermin!'

She loved all animals but had suffered the same systematic brain washing to which we have all been subject since childhood: that anything with teeth or talons is vermin. This belief is now refuted by hundreds of sound scientific investigations, and I put on my educator's hat and went into lengthy details about why weasels, and their larger cousins stoats, are such an integral, essential part of the fragile natural balance. Far too many of our main-line predators, such as polecats, pine martens, otters and birds of prey, have been blasted, trapped and snared to extinction in favour of game farming. Now that we have a plethora of rats, mice, rabbits and squirrels, can the keepers see how they have messed things up? Every year landowners spend a fortune on poisons, ammunition and traps, whereas if the natural predators had been allowed to survive there would be a perfect harmony with not too many of any one species. It is an established fact that pine martens are the only efficient way of keeping squirrels under control, yet do the Forestry Commission, for instance, introduce them to their woods? No, of course they don't. They just keep putting more

How can the weasel be called 'vermin'?

and more poison and traps down, which have little effect on the squirrels but kill plenty of woodmice, voles and birds, as well as the stoats, weasels and owls at the top of the food chain.

The weasels we take in at the Hospital are usually orphans whose parents have been persecuted and killed. When young they are tiny soft little creatures not much bigger than a mouse. They never grow very big but they have tremendous courage and will readily attack animals many, many times larger than themselves, including man. Their spirit and wildness are renowned; like intelligent sparrowhawks they never bow to tameness and captivity.

As they grow larger at the Hospital their movements become so fast that it is impossible to handle them. When they are ready for release I usually take the cage out to a suitably secluded site, open the door and watch the blur of speed disappear into the long grass.

Being nature's hunters, stoats and weasels must be in possession of all their faculties otherwise they would starve in the hard world of the predator. Consequently, a stoat almost blinded in a car accident had to stay on at the Hospital. Quite unlike birds, which have little or no sense of smell, a blind mammal can cope quite well in captivity but – with the exception of a few cases such as seals – would not last long in the wild. Sebastian, or Spartacus (we never could agree on a name), has a specially constructed pen where he is familiar with every square inch and passing sound. He lies for hours with his tongue poking through the wire front of his cage and rested for some reason on the metal of the door catch. Perhaps it tastes nice – we will never know. But I wish he wouldn't do it for he looks dead and has shocked many a visitor by just lying there, staring. We have always hoped that a female stoat might materialise, but stoats are becoming so scarce that we see only one casualty a year and all of them since Sebastian have been releasable.

However, the real king of the weasel tribe, the Mustelidae, is the badger. He alone of the family has resisted the incursions of man. In fact, his attitude has been to steer well clear of any disturbance on his territory. Badger numbers were keeping quite high until the Ministry of Agriculture, Fisheries and Food started wide-scale gassing of setts, followed closely by a recent upsurge in trapping badgers for sale to field sportsmen.

The Cook Report, an independent television programme, was producing an in-depth documentary on the horrors of using badgers for sport. They had made contact with many other badger and conservation groups but had been unable to film any live badgers which had been injured for sport. As we, at St Tiggywinkles, are one of very few groups which actually save individual wild animals, it was obvious that they should come to us for footage.

At that time we had no injured badgers at the Hospital and although we have two resident badgers, Biddy and Granny, there was no way I would let these tame badgers be filmed. Our arrangement with *The Cook Report* was that if a baited casualty came in I would phone immediately.

As it was, I did not need to call them, for every day, two or three times a day, they would phone frantically to see if anything had happened.

Then, with just two days to go before transmission, I received the terrible phone call which told me that a badly injured badger had been seen, crying out, under a hedge on the outskirts of town. I left immediately to recover the badger, asking Sue to put Peter Salkeld of *The Cook Report* on stand-by as this sounded like a baiting incident. Sue would explain that if the badger needed urgent medical attention this would be given as soon as the vet arrived, whether the film crew were there or not. In fact, they arranged for a freelance cameraman who lived near by to get there as fast as possible.

The cameraman and the vet arrived at the same time. I had laid the badger, which was still whickering, in the chalet at the back of the garden. The vet assured us that the cries were of delirium more than pain. For once, under the eagle eye of a camera, we could show some of the horrors that we see regularly inflicted on our deer, badgers and foxes. But first of all we had to attempt to save the animal's life.

The badger, although nearly comatose, continued screaming. Its wounds were large and grossly infected and to top it all we had to take the precaution of muzzling it with a bandage while we inserted an intravenous drip in the cephalic vein of one of its front legs. A whole range of drugs were injected to counter infection, shock and pain, and then to cap it all and increase the unfortunate creature's indignity we had to fit the badger with a plastic collar to protect the intravenous connection from damage should the badger come round.

The whole programme was an indictment of those who kill for sport and our poor badger at last showed to Britain some of the traumas which we see every day. The badger, not unexpectedly, died without regaining consciousness, but it seemed that the whole of Britain had seen his struggle to live and now questions were heard in Parliament about the effectiveness of badger legislation. Many of the animal welfare groups used *The Cook Report* as a campaign platform to raise members and funds, all of which was good news for badgers. Peter Salkeld told us that our efforts and the sight of that unfortunate badger really made the programme hit home, so perhaps the poor creature didn't die in vain.

When the BBC were making a programme on a similar subject, they began by filming a badger group using light aircraft to patrol setts in their area. They managed to get plenty of film of aeroplanes, badger watchers and setts but – you have guessed it – no badgers.

Coincidentally, we were treating a badger which had been rescued from the same area. It had been severed nearly in half by a snare which unfortunately is a legitimate weapon of the gamekeeper. The snare had dug in below the badger's front legs and had cut deeply into its chest, stopping only when the bones of its front legs and ribs got in the way. (Incidentally, Nicholas Ridley, the Government Minister responsible for wildlife legislation, had recently been quoted as saying that snares were not cruel. He should have been with us as we tried to stitch the two halves of this badger together.)

With plenty of tlc (tender loving care) the badger recovered and very soon the massive wound was only a small snick. Once more a television company had to rely on our work to bring realism to their programme, and we agreed to release the now fully fit badger back to its own territory in front of the cameras.

I drove 60 kilometres to the release site and tried to give the director an idea of what would happen when I opened the basket. In fact I described how the badger would amble off towards its sett, giving the cameras plenty of 'wobbly bottom' to film as it disappeared into the gloom on the night. Once again the best laid plans were sabotaged by a determined animal – the badger bounded into the distance like a lively buck hare with the cameraman leaping along behind.

The badger filmed by the BBC had been saved not just by surgical intervention but also by the use of some sophisticated drugs now becoming available for use with animals.

Take Lasix for instance. This is the registered trade name of a preparation of frusemide, a diuretic aimed at alleviating pulmonary oedema. A diuretic causes the kidneys to get rid of more water, thus drying up excess fluid (oedema) especially in the chest. It has proved especially important in clearing the oedema which often follows road traffic accidents. Its efficacy was drummed home to me by the case of a large boar badger knocked unconscious by a car at Cuddington, a village about 5 kilometres out of Aylesbury. Incidentally, we named him Brockie for ease of identification.

On arrival at the Hospital, his condition was obviously critical: his whole metabolism was shutting down. Usually in this situation we would have put him on an intravenous drip, but his breathing was so laboured and his chest so bubbling that we dared not introduce any more fluid for fear of drowning him.

I laid Brockie out flat in the incubator as he gasped unconsciously for breath. He was not going to make it, but, since our motto could well be 'Where there's life there's hope', we set to, giving him the benefits of all we had learned with other badgers.

He did not move as we injected the Lasix to clear the pulmonary oedema. He had obviously been hit on the head – hence his unconsciousness – and our injection of dexamethasone would relieve some of the pressure inside his skull. It would also assist his breathing, as would a third drug, etamiphylline camsylate. As steroids like dexamethasone can inhibit the healing process we also had to institute a course of antibiotics. I did not expect Brockie to last

Brockie was fed with liquid food.

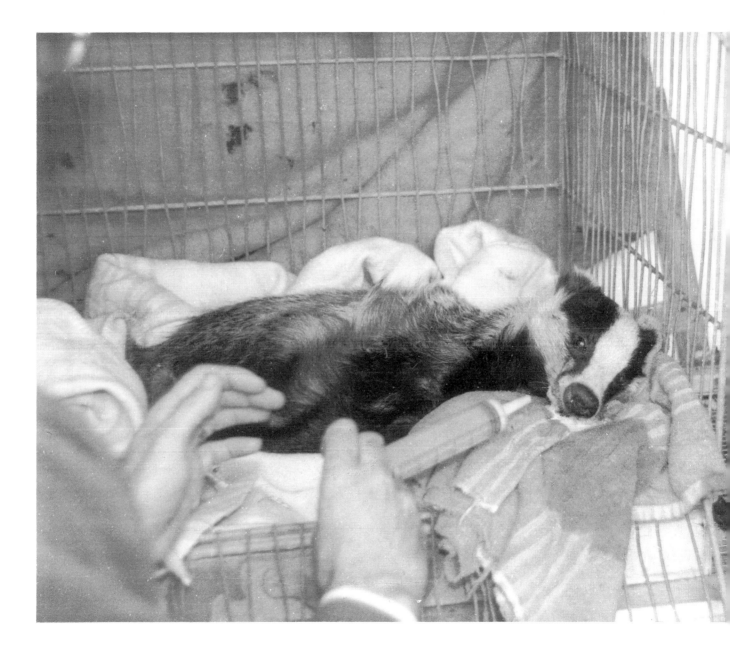

until the morning, but at least he was warm and comfortable in the incubator – not that he knew much about it.

Three times I went out to him during the night and each time he was still breathing. I got up in the morning knowing he could not possibly have survived, and so I went down to turn off the incubator. As I reached across I could see that he was no longer gasping but was breathing steadily. He was alive and his condition was nowhere near as critical as it had been the evening before.

Having cleared the fluid from his lungs, exactly the opposite situation could start to arise. He would gradually dehydrate unless I could get some fluids into him. An intravenous drip was out of the question as it would only flood his lungs again. I was perplexed as to which course to take but Brockie, who all this time had been out to the world, gave me a sign: he blinked one tiny button eye. He appeared totally paralysed, but if he could swallow I might be able to get some Lectade into him.

I generally keep long-nozzled 60-millilitre syringes for this purpose. The nozzle kept my fingers away from his jaws in case he could snap them shut. He made no objection as I gently lifted his head onto a makeshift pillow of towels – these would soak up any overflow to save getting his Vet-bed unnecessarily wet. Carefully I slid the nozzle into the side of his mouth and let the first Lectade trickle between his teeth. His tongue sensed the sweet liquid and I could see the swallow-reflex as it went down. Great. All I needed now was patience and a lot of luck.

Every two hours I went to him and trickled 60 millilitres of Lectade between his teeth. For the first few liquid feeds he could not even move his jaws but gradually he came to expect the drink. His bottom jaw started to move in unison with his swallowing, and I could hear those formidable teeth grinding past each other. He was on the mend, but just how far he would improve was anyone's guess.

Brockie accepted my manhandling when feeding and cleaning him without so much as a snarl, and I took his passiveness to be the result of his concussion. After all, I had always thought that no wild animal since Androcles's lion had ever appreciated being helped. However, one morning, as I was pipette-feeding him, he saw Sue approaching the chalet where his incubator was plugged in. His deep, low growl, obviously directed at her, made me jump back in a standard animal handler's self-protective reaction. I would not have believed it but clearly he knew I was helping him and was actually letting me handle him without so much as a cross word.

It was three weeks before he could even move his head but as long as there was a daily improvement, no matter how slight, it was worth continuing my intensive nursing. However, as is the case with all patients with major head injuries, he could have just died at any moment.

I had to be ready for that, just in case I became too attached to him.

I was by then supplementing his Lectade with a complete liquid food, Ensure. He loved the egg-nog flavour and would let me hold his head in the bowl as he lapped it up all by himself. Every day saw some improvement; after four weeks I was reasonably confident and terribly relieved that I would not have to ask the vet to put Brockie to sleep. I took him out of his incubator and introduced him to a cage with an overhead heater. He was starting to move around, rather drunkenly, but it was a step in the right direction.

Brockie has been with me for four months and although he now takes solid food he has not quite got it together and tends to sway from side to side on uncoordinated hind legs. Mind you, his front end is now perfect, forcing me to take extreme care when handling him. Gone is the *entente cordiale* of his helplessness: he is fast becoming a wild animal again. I am not sure if he will ever be strong enough for release but if not he will be able to move in with Granny and Biddy in the special area we are setting aside for them in the new St Tiggywinkles.

Thankfully, many of our badger rescues are just that – a rescue with immediate release. The predicaments badgers get into make even hedgehogs look bright. I have just rescued a badger from a pit. Sounds ominous, doesn't it? But no, this badger had to find the only First World War gun emplacement in the country that had not been filled in. Having negotiated

A badger, happy to have torn off his bandages.

the thick scrub beside Ashridge golf course, I had to climb down and join her in the pit before catching her and passing her up to Andy. We released her on the 14th green, from where she could amble back to her sett.

Another badger appeared out of the early morning mist at a school just outside Aylesbury. The young schoolchildren spotted the apparition in a goal mouth on the school playing field, but as the morning was so damp with mist they could not make out what was there. Only a wary approach by one of the schoolteachers revealed a very irate badger hopelessly entangled in the school's brand new goal netting. I was called at the same time as Richard Duggan, the photographer for the local newspaper. He obviously wanted some action shots as I unravelled the badger. But I am a bit wiser than that and wrestling with a very much awake and grumpy badger was not my idea of fun.

In its throes to get out of the net the badger had worn a great ring of flattened mud. He was in a fine mess. My approach had to be intricately planned and executed. First I used my grasper to noose his neck and hold him secure, and then I pushed him, and the football net around him, into my carrying basket. Finally, with great forethought and infinite care, I hacked a great hole in the brand new netting.

My next manoeuvre was to take the whole lot – badger, basket, netting and mud – down to the surgery where the vet could anaesthetise my captive and then we could unravel him. Easy. The next morning we released the badger.

This time he met no hindrance on the way and waddled straight for an invisible track through the school boundary hedge back to more familiar territory.

We have seen badgers at close quarters for many years. We have seen the terrible things that happen to them. But the British people at large were unaware of the plight of these animals until a champion came on the scene and graphically told the story of the badgers' flight from man. Tragically the whole of Britain, and Britain's wildlife, lost this champion when Aeron Clement died early in 1989. Aeron had taken the world by storm with the publication of *The Cold Moons*. Here was a giant voice for wildlife, a shining bold light in the gloom that is protection for wild mammals in this country. Even when Aeron knew that he was very ill, he continued to toil ceaselessly and selflessly for his beliefs. We shall miss him and I know that the animals will miss him but at the sad occasion of his funeral at St Teilo's Church, overlooking his beloved Welsh valley at Llandeilo, Aeron had left this message:

I, who was born to die
Shall live so that the world of animals and man
    shall come together –
I shall live

An Inuk proverb

The early months of 1989 were mild throughout Britain giving all the small mammals and birds, especially the tiny wrens, long-tailed tits and resident warblers, a helping hand into the new year. Usually we are called on to treat very few hedgehogs in the winter, and those that we do have at the Hospital are hibernating in outside pens, fit and ready for release in April and May. But this particular year they all stayed awake, which was good news for their survival but played havoc with our food bills and prevented us carrying out our normal routine maintenance. Amazingly, we got through about 250 tins of dog food each week. Exceptionally, in January the first baby bird of the year was brought in.

The telephone rang with requests for advice on hedgehogs which were still out and about getting injured, instead of in hibernation. We were helping with the rearing of a litter of leverets in the first week of February.

Our pens were full and close to overflowing. No, I will not say full, for that implies that we could not take any more casualties. Hedgehogs can always be tucked in somewhere and even foxes and badgers can be temporarily housed in collapsible, portable Majestic cage pens, generously given to us by Shaw and Sons of Aston Clinton. We will always take an animal, even if it means erecting fresh housing in the middle of the night – though of course we try not to disturb the neighbours.

Although for the previous ten years I had always built the pens and aviaries myself, a recent incident told me that it was about time I hired professionals: DIY and I do not agree. One evening I was in the garage, ready to do some woodwork. I had pulled out my Black and Decker Workmate, a portable bench that is absolutely essential for all manner of carpentry work. However, as I opened it to set it up, it caught my little finger in the hinges and clicked into place, erected. Now, to collapse a Workmate you need both hands, but my left hand was trapped and beginning to throb. I tapped frantically on the wall, hoping Sue would hear me and rescue me. For twenty minutes I banged away, apparently, as Sue told me later, giving the impression that I was working hard and fixing things to the wall. My finger was going blue and numb – things were getting drastic. I shouted but nobody could hear me. I tried to carry the Workmate suspended from my poor little finger but I was trapped at a ridiculous angle across the top of the bench. By then, I must admit, I was losing my temper. Then I had a brainwave. Stretching as far as I could enabled me to hook a foot in the top of my tool box. Dragging it towards me I found a screwdriver and some spanners and took the Workmate to bits, at last releasing my horribly flat finger.

After that I decided to let someone who knew what he was doing carry out our maintenance and construction work. Maurice Fromes, a good friend, came along and painted the outside of the house, a job that had needed doing for some time, and he fitted an outer door at the front of our porch, making a little reception area for casualties. His latest task was to box in one of the back doors and raise the floor with concrete to create a small conservatory which

would take one of the freezers we use for storing animal food.

After two days he had fitted the walls and laid the concrete, which we would have to avoid for a few days to let it set. Late in the evening as I was doing my final rounds I noticed that two of our three dinosaur footprints were missing – yes, real fossilised dinosaur footprints, revealing where the monsters had walked in soft mud one hundred and fifty million years ago in the Jurassic period. Sue and I had collected the enormous pieces of rock some years before at a quarry in Dorset. To us they were irreplaceable.

Sue reassured me 'Nobody could have moved them. They were far too heavy.'

I followed her indoors, and we stepped over the setting concrete floor as we went.

A horrifying thought dawned on me as I was at full stretch between the back step and the new doorway. I suddenly had a mental picture of Maurice searching for ballast and hardcore earlier that day.

Sue phoned Maurice.

'Crikey,' he said. 'I thought I was doing you a favour getting rid of those old rocks. I'll be right over.'

It was a very understandable mistake. After all, how many people have dinosaur footprints tucked away in the corner of their garden?

Maurice was terribly apologetic and, taking up a pickaxe, started chipping away at his concrete flooring.

Digging for dinosaur fossils.

'I think one of them is about here,' he said, levering up something solid.

'What about the other?' I asked.

'I hate to tell you this,' he replied, but you know I said that I had broken your sledge-hammer? Well, I broke it trying to break up the other rock. It's now in dozens of pieces.'

Sue appeared with a camera to record, presumably for posterity, two grown men digging in concrete for dinosaur fossils, at twelve o'clock at night.

By now Sue and I could see the funny side of the situation. We did manage to retrieve the iguanodon footprint which, when hosed off, seemed undamaged by its second interment. The other pieces we left in the concrete so that some future archaeologist would think that dinosaurs once walked in Pemberton Close.

Even at this time of night an inevitable cardboard box arrived at the front porch. The smartly dressed lady told us how she had found the 'hare' lying in one of her fields. She was very insistent, to the point of being aggressive, that it be returned to her for release on her land – apparently, the beagle hunt only marauded on the other side of the road. I suppose she thought we could train the 'hare', to stay in the safety of her property. Anyway Sue, now getting a little insistent herself, explained the anomalies of the Veterinary Surgeons Act, which prohibits us from treating animals and returning them to, what is in law, the owner. For the 'hare's' sake a truce was arrived at and we took the animal in. We had not even looked at it. When she was gone I opened the box to find not a hare but a rabbit and I wondered if she would want it returned after all. I had my doubts, even though it eats exactly the same food as a hare.

Of course I was right. She could not hang up quickly enough when she heard that her 'hare' was a rabbit. This is another example of the double standards applied to British wildlife by some groups of the population.

Unfortunately this double standard is being forced on Britain by the contradiction in terms 'shooting for conservation'. What a joke. We all know that every species doomed to extinction is in this position as a direct result of man's indiscriminate killing. I know that shotgun users tell us they only shoot pheasants or grouse or ducks, but, believe me, apart from slaughtering these species, the guns shoot anything that moves. I know. I am in the front-line field hospital for those birds lucky, or unlucky, enough to escape by being maimed and not killed.

One thing that really worries me is that the Nature Conservancy Council, the Government body which advises on wildlife, is now giving grants for wildfowlers (men that make a sport out of shooting ducks) to buy land frequented by their quarry. The argument is that without the hunters there would be nobody to protect the copses, hedgerows and woodlands from rapacious farmers. It strikes me as a licence to accept murder to prevent rape. A Government with any teeth would merely have to introduce legislation for the better protection of covies for wildlife just as groups such as the League against Cruel Sports

DON'T

Don't feed hedgehogs on cows' milk (tinned dog food or cat food is much better)

Don't give milk or bread to baby birds (tinned dog or cat food is much better)

Don't give brandy to birds, and don't give any liquids to them orally

Don't use aerosols to kill fleas or other parasites (use a safe pyretheum powder)

Don't attempt to stroke a wild animal (it will bite)

Don't attempt to wash an oiled bird (take it to an expert)

Don't keep a wild animal as a pet

Don't handle young mammals (mum is around)

Don't pick up baby birds unless they are injured (the parents will be near by)

and the Royal Society for the Protection of Birds have done on their own reserves.

In fact it is getting even more ridiculous, with the NCC now saying that it will not give grants to buy land unless the traditional historic uses (which include foxhunting) are maintained.

Some people say to me that they prefer

animals to humans. I may have thought that way a few years ago but now everybody we seem to meet is a genuine caring human being. Some are wonderfully eccentric in their concern for both animals and humans. One kindly old gentleman who lived on the south coast would write to us regularly about the little invisible men who lived on Venus. They were going to come to earth to eat up all the motor cars which kill and injure children as well as animals – a wonderful sentiment, but unfortunately they were as much a part of the world of fantasy as the Warriors of the Rainbow, who according to American mythology was to come to save all the animals. I wish it were true.

Others are much more down to earth. A traveller, a man of the road, had saved £1.95 for the Wildlife Hospital Trust. Without the wherewithal to get it to Aylesbury, he asked a man he met in a wood if he would make sure we received it. Out of the blue the gentleman wrote a cheque to cover the £1.95, but when he posted it he added another £500 on the strength that the traveller had faith enough to send us his last pennies.

All the time the generosity of people confirms my faith in the human race in spite of those few who shoot, kill and maim for sport. Many even go to great efforts to arrange fundraising functions on behalf of our patients. Wherever possible, Sue and I try to get along to these and support the organisers.

As people see that we are taking in and caring for more and more animals, so they are responding with donations. We can do any amount of work, seven days a week, twenty-four hours a day, but we still need funds to buy food and drugs and, of course, to build the new Hospital. With all these good people behind us we are now showing the rest of the world that wild animals can, and should, be saved. With their backing we have changed so many attitudes and now an increasing number of people are 'having a go' and succeeding. I really do think that, because of this, wildlife has a much better future. And perhaps, eventually, those people who hunt and shoot our wildlife will themselves become extinct.

10 Hooked Beaks and Needle-sharp Talons

It's so easy to get the names wrong, especially with some of the immature birds which all look like peas in a pod. Even when you do get the name right there can still be confusion, especially to the baffled finder. I do not know how many times somebody has brought in an owl of the species *Athene noctua*. They ask which type of owl it is, to which we reply correctly, giving its popular name, 'little owl'.

'We can see it's a little owl, but which *species* is it?'

We try to explain. 'That's what it's called, the little owl.'

There are so many silly names that plague the British list: the majority of blackbirds seem to be either females, who are brown, or young birds, who are speckled, not unlike a thrush. Grey squirrels come in all colours from very red to black or white (including, of course, grey). The mute swan has a whole barrage of noises which it can and will utter, especially if you are trying to catch it. But perhaps the most ridiculously named of all are the long- and short-eared owls, whose ears are merely holes in the side of their heads and nothing at all to do with the raised feathers on their crowns which give them their names.

Short-eared owls are winter visitors to Britain and do not often get taken into rescue centres, whereas long-eared owls are regular inmates of centres along the eastern half of England. Along with these two species there are only three others that can be expected at rescue centres: the barn, the tawny and, of course, the little owls. Snowy and eagle owls are not native to Britain, and any we come up against will probably have escaped from captivity.

Barn owls are now comparatively scarce but the little owls seem to be doing very well. They are bold birds which stare defiance at anyone trying to handle them. Just like weasels they do not seem to feel fear and are brave beyond the call of duty. One female was sitting on her eggs in a hollow tree when a forester started to fell it. The chain saw cut deeper and deeper into the tree but she would not move. Only when the leading edge of the blade cut into her wing did she attempt to escape. But by then her left wing

The little owl appears forever disgruntled.

was irreparably damaged and consequently she now shares one of our aviaries with any other little owls passing through.

The devotion of the little owls as parents is becoming well known as more and more people, especially bird ringers, come into contact with them.* We have another resident little owl, this time a young bird who, it seemed, had fallen from the nest when newly hatched and become entangled in a twisted root. Unable to escape he must have been there for some weeks, with his devoted parents taking him food. Eventually he was found and brought to us but by then the bones of one leg and a wing had become fused and deformed. He could never be released.

However, even though he was a very young bird he still spat in defiance at us when he arrived, and he would produce as loud a hiss as any irate mute swan. This hissing is apparently identical to the warning sound of the American burrowing owl. A researcher in zoology from the United States heard about Wilfred's antics. He had tried the world over to record a young owl's warning hiss but it seemed that the owl in our garage was the only one that would oblige.

The intrepid researcher came all the way to Aylesbury just to record Wilfred. He told us the hiss was thought to imitate that of a snake – a sure way for these little owls to keep would-be predators away from their burrow nests. No, I

mean 'these small owls', although little owls do often nest in burrows. He was enthralled as Wilfred stared, glared and hissed on demand. For nearly an hour we sat in the garage and taped until our American guest had to catch the return snail-train from Aylesbury to London. I ran him to the station, and asked if he would send a copy of the tape from America.

One hour and ten minutes later a frantic phone call told us that Bill, the researcher, while being shaken to bits on the train, had played back his very rare recording. Not a thing. Nothing at all. It appears to me that this is quite a common fault with these complicated recording machines, but however it had happened it had not registered any of the little owl's defiance. Bill asked if he could come back up on the next train and have another go.

One hour and fifteen minutes later Bill arrived, travel weary, back in Aylesbury. I picked him up from the station and this time made sure that his recording was perfect. Afterwards I drove him back to the station. To this day I don't know whether he made it back to America with Wilfred's hiss.

Quite unlike little owls, tawny owls are the epitome of everything one imagines an owl to be. Quite large, with thick downy plumage and enormous dark languid eyes which blink at you behind faded light blue eyelids, these are the owls of the ghastly scream or ghostly hoot – the 'tu-whit to-who', as Shakespeare would have us believe. Contrary to public opinion, owls are not all that wise. In fact they are as thick as two

* Bird ringers are enthusiasts licensed by the British Trust for Ornithology to put numbered metal rings on the legs of wild birds. Any recovered rings give an insight into migration and territorial patterns of wild birds.

A typically fluffy tawny owl chick – this one with a broken leg.

short planks, which is the main reason why every year finds us taking in dozens that have landed themselves in trouble in one way or another.

They arrive in all shapes and sizes and in various conditions, from the gorgeous fluff balls that are orphans to the large aggressive adult females who can pierce your hand to the bone with their tremendously sharp and powerful talons. But I have a little trick up my sleeve: if you lay an adult tawny on its back, hold its legs to contain those talons and then tickle it under an ear, it will more than likely doze off like a baby, allowing you to check for injury all over its body. Put it up the right way again and it will attack you, if you let it.

Tawnies are terrible road users. They see a mouse and off they go, completely ignoring any traffic until it hits them. We take in dozens every year from motorists who are as shocked as the casualty by the impact of such a large bird on the windscreen. We even took in a tawny which had crashed through the window of one of those Marylebone to Aylesbury trains.

In many cases, because of the great padding effect of an owl's feathers, the injury is only a simple concussion, although this may take a week to recede. Quite often there is the loss of an eye but as tawny owls tend to hunt by sound, pinpointed by their asymmetrically positioned ears, this does not cause them too much of a

problem. Then there are broken wings and legs, as in the case of a tawny caught in the roof rack of a speeding car, unbeknown to the driver. Most injuries heal perfectly and the owls are released back into the wild. However, those which cannot be released are kept in conditions as natural as we can make them. They are also encouraged to mate so that their progeny can take their parents' place back in owl society.

A really dense layer of feathers can often save the life of a bird where a mammal of a similar size would not stand a chance, especially in a collision with a motor vehicle. One cock pheasant we took in had been hit by a car travelling at 80 kilometres an hour in Amersham, 25 kilometres from Aylesbury. At the site of the accident there was no sign of the pheasant so the driver continued his speedy journey towards Aylesbury. When he arrived he thought of checking for damage caused by the collision. What he found was an enormous hole in his radiator grill and behind it a nonplussed cock pheasant sitting looking at him from in front of the radiator itself. The bird had broken a wing and a leg but with simple splinting these soon healed and he was released on Sally's farm, well away from both roads and shooters.

We try to treat every bird species with the same degree of care, whether it be an owl, pheasant or sparrow. We never see any of the larger exotic birds of prey which might just warrant a bit of VIP treatment. Peregrines and

This cock pheasant soon recovered his dignity, if not his tail.

eagles are very much restricted to the higher ground of northern England and Scotland, while the majestic buzzard (a different species from the macabre scavenger of the Western movies) thrives, once again, in the north as well as in Wales and the west of England. Our one and only peregrine call was from a Chief Inspector (since retired) of the RSPCA, who had picked up an injured bird close to Oxford. I was semi-unprepared for the arrival of a large falcon. I certainly did not have any of those flash and fancy falconry gloves used for handling these exotic birds. However, I had my faithful welder's gloves, and decided they would have to do even if they did dent the dignity of the bird.

I must admit that the falcon really was a majestic creature, as it stood looking very disdainful at being confined to a cat basket. It wasn't a peregrine but I knew it was one of a number of species of falcons which are imported from the Middle East and Pakistan. There was an official ring on its leg and so I could ascertain that it was a captive bird which had escaped and could also track down the owner.

By coincidence I was due, that weekend, for the regular inspection of the Schedule 4 birds then in the Hospital and my official records of those I had recently treated. To take in any of the birds contained on Schedule 4 of the Wildlife and Countryside Act you have to be licensed by the Department of the Environment as, wait for it, a Licensed Rehabilitation Keeper. As such, scheduled birds are referred to you and records are kept on DoE form 14100. After six weeks, if the birds cannot be released, the DoE form 14085 is used to register it at the Bristol headquarters; from here is sent a plastic ring to mark the bird.

Among my Schedule 4 birds was a constant flow of kestrels and sparrowhawks, together with kingfishers, redwings, fieldfares, a wryneck and the occasional black- or red-throated diver. However, the large falcon sitting aloof in a corner aviary really stopped the inspector in his tracks. Luckily he could identify it as a lugger, or lanner falcon, and he even went to the trouble of finding the owner for me. It seemed that it had escaped some days before from Guilsborough Grange Wildlife Park in Northamptonshire. After a quick phone call a much relieved Keeper of Birds drove down to recover his absentee and paid us a handsome reward of £10.

This bird was very lucky to be found alive as most escaped falconry birds do not have the wherewithal to survive in the wild. Those that escape with their jesses, leash and bells still attached are doomed at the first snag they meet. I have just recently taken in my first ever buzzard, a beautiful bird whose soft friendly mewing betrayed his closeness to man and belied the horrible things which had happened to his legs.

He had obviously escaped with his jesses, bell, swivel and leash still attached, flapping behind as he flew – a time-bomb ready to devastate. And sure enough it did so – the leash became entangled on a barbed wire fence and in struggling to free itself the buzzard managed to break both his legs. By the time he was found they were splintered to smithereens, the bones sticking crazily out at all angles. He must have been suffering for days as the open wounds were under attack from an army of maggots.

Although against the rules I had no hesitation in immediately cutting the DoE ring and jesses off those tortured legs. This really was a case that needed a miracle or at least skilful veterinary intervention.

The vet needed to anaesthetise the bird, and this required us to weigh him on the surgery's kitchen scales. He really was a lovely, friendly bird and sat on the scales calling gently to us. As usual, we referred to Cole's *Avian Medicine and Surgery* for the right dose of the right anaesthetic. The vet measured it off, checked his calculations and injected. The bird slept.

We each worked on a leg, cleaning away the mess and maggots with diluted Savlon. Rather than risk the possibility of introducing any further infection by pinning the legs, the vet splinted and bandaged them. Then all of a sudden the bird stopped breathing. We tried in vain to bring it round but, no, it had died there on the operating table. Losing that magnificent bird really hurt but we had done everything by the book. Perhaps those days gibbeted on a barbed wire fence had been too much for the buzzard's heart. Really it was the keeper who had let it escape who should feel guilt at the way

The buzzard had escaped from its owner, still wearing jesses, bell, swivel and leash.

the bird had suffered.

Most genuine practitioners of the art of falconry would rather die than let their bird escape with a leash attached. To them their bird is an extension of themselves, a close friend who receives only the best attention. A falconer's bird is always in tip-top condition – there is never a feather out of place or broken. Also, with the regulations now in force, regular inspection soon picks up anything untoward happening to a bird. However, in all walks of life, a person operating outside the law often fails to keep up to standard, and this is particularly the case when it comes to the clandestine keeping of protected birds.

On one occasion two kestrels which had just been confiscated from an illegal keeper were brought to us by the police. Their feathers were matted, broken and soiled with their own droppings, and the normally bright, sparkling eyes of my favourite birds were dull and lifeless. These two had been kept in an Ali Baba laundry basket. They had not seen the light of day for some time and I doubt if they had ever had a chance to bathe, one of the great delights of any bird.

In a warm flight cage they did not hesitate to jump into the large bowl of water and were soon rocking backwards and forwards, with feathers fluffed out just like animated cuddly toys and

LEFT *The two confiscated kestrels brought to the Hospital by the police.*

RIGHT *Purdie – the first bird the Stockers took in.*

disguising the hunting birds they really were.

Purdie, the kestrel I took in at the very beginning when we first started looking after wild creatures twelve years ago, still loves her baths, but unlike these two birds which had been taken from the wild she cannot be released. Instead, she lives a reasonably full life along with Steed, a male kestrel who for some unknown reason does not grow full length primary feathers in his right wing. His flying prowess is limited to short hops of about 10 metres, about 2 metres off the ground. But there is nothing wrong with his sexual prowess and over the last five years he and Purdie have produced thirty-five young kestrels for release. As far as we know these young birds have been successful in the wild. Of all the rings fitted to them, only one has been returned. This was a full six months after release when the young bird was killed inside a factory chimney in Essex. Of course we cannot assume that if a bird is killed its corpse will be found or the ring returned. However, though only a small proportion of wild kestrel young survive their first winter, I believe that our releases are much better fed than those reared in the wild and are consequently much more resilient to inclement weather.

As well as being superb natural parents, Purdie and Steed are also highly competent foster parents to any orphaned kestrels that come in. The advantage of having adult birds rear orphans is that the young birds do not

The male kestrel Steed, Purdie's handsome mate.

become imprinted on humans and can go on to lead a totally natural life in the wild. So diligent are the adults in feeding their charges that they have often raised nine youngsters in a season.

Purdie is twelve this year and as the oldest kestrel known was just over sixteen years of age, I know she could pass away at any time. Meanwhile, Steed has started this season's food passing, a behaviour that reinforces the pair bond. This is a sure sign that once more Purdie will soon be laying eggs on the floor of their aviary. Most kestrels like to nest in trees or old buildings or, when in an aviary, in a nest box. But not Purdie. She thinks that she is a merlin and sticks rigidly to the ground level nest sites, even though I have tried lifting her eggs into the box. The only worry is that an itinerant hedgehog will blunder into her aviary and disturb her while she is brooding. Mind you, Purdie's alarm call can be heard half a kilometre away and she does not hesitate to scream at anything with four legs; she will, no doubt, let me know if there is an intruder.

Usually the kestrels we receive are either orphans or injured, but four brown speckled eggs were exposed to the elements when a farmer in High Wycombe dismantled a hay rick. As there was no way of rebuilding the site, we had to take drastic measures to save the unhatched kestrels. One of our ambulances, equipped with hot water bottles, was despatched immediately to retrieve the eggs. Purdie could not in fairness be asked to raise these four with her own, and so for the time being I set up the small incubator I had

Orphan kestrels reared by Steed and Purdie.

used to hatch quail eggs when we had kept these small ground birds.

In the next aviary to Purdie was Nika, a lovely female kestrel. Nika had taken to laying infertile eggs and would fuss around her house-keeping, moving her eggs to and fro and then settling them under her, 'chucking' to herself in pleasure. When she was off her eggs feeding I very quickly replaced them with the four hay rick eggs. She never noticed the difference except that after a few more days incubation she could possibly hear the babies 'kicking' inside the shells.

I am always enchanted by the way the fierce birds of prey, from eagles to kestrels, show supreme gentleness in tearing off small morsels of meat and feeding them to their youngsters. Nika would spend most of the day, just like Purdie, leaning over her new-found family, giving them the tiniest portions of day-old chick or mouse.

You can almost see kestrel chicks growing, so fast is the transition from bundle of fluff to sleek brown bird. Nika's youngsters were soon flying around the aviary after their 'mother', stealing every mouse or chick she picked up. After sixteen weeks I could let all five of them go, but left food available just in case they wanted to come back. I vividly remember one kestrel chick staying around for three months, roosting every night on the next door neighbour's burglar alarm.

All the birds of prey we release are quite capable of looking after themselves in the wild. It's only the escapees which suffer. I recently rescued another falconer's bird, this time a kestrel, complete with jesses. It had taken sanctuary inside the stores at Stoke Mandeville Hospital, just across the railway from us.

She was noticeably undernourished but once I had put her into an aviary she could share with some hedgehogs, I offered a choice of menu: freshly defrosted chick or mouse.*

A pair of Little owls

* These we buy frozen. They are the surplus cullings from breeders and would be thrown away if they were not bought to feed birds of prey and other meat-eating animals.

However, in a reaction that possibly reflected her upbringing in captivity, she flew down to the hedgehogs' bowl of dog food, sat on the brim and merrily tucked in to Luda Dog Food with Liver – great nourishment for hedgehogs but of doubtful quality for a bird of prey.

It took some weeks to wean her from the habit. Through the Department of the Environment we have notified her owner that we have his bird and we are still waiting for him to turn up.

11 Finicky Feeding

It's fairly obvious that a hooked beak is adapted for tearing meat. With most other beak shapes it's also possible to have a pretty good guess at a bird's diet. A situation guaranteed to make me rampage through intensive care was when birds had been given the wrong food by new volunteers. I do not know how many times I have had to take corn away from insect-eating blackbirds to swap it with a bowl of maggots being totally ignored by starving finches. Thankfully most species are either seed-eater or soft-bill (insect-eater). However, some casualties are so specialised that a rescue centre really has to rack its brains to find a way of feeding that both provides nourishment and is acceptable to the bird.

Swifts are regular patients at rescue centres. Their beaks are wide and soft, quite incapable of actually pecking up food: they catch insects in their gaping mouths as they wheel through the sky at breakneck speeds. Di Conger in Washington has had great success this year in hand-feeding chimney swifts, a very similar American species. The secret of her success was undoubtedly her infinite patience; but she also had the knack of getting food into open mouths with a syringe.

A species which could almost be a giant swift is the now very scarce nightjar (closely related to the whip-poor-will in America). This is also a gaping feeder, using its cavernous mouth to trawl night insects and moths from the air. One we had in this year was successfully fed by syringe on a mixture of 'Glop' and dried insects. It was an absolutely amazing bird, with the most delicately marked soft plumage and a head that disappeared each time it opened its enormous mouth.

Even more ridiculous than swift or nightjar beaks are the often overlength but, no doubt, practical probing beaks of the waders. There seems to be no way of force-feeding them as we could the nightjar since I am sure their beaks would bend at the slightest pressure. We have had to rely on their feeding themselves and we have tried to create a suitable environment in an aquarium by providing 8 to 10 centimetres of leaf litter floor and two deep plastic cups, one holding maggots and the other holding water. Sometimes a bird would use these cups immediately, but on most occasions the wader would

The rare nightjar had a broken wing.

CAPTIVE WILD CREATURE DIETS

Baby Birds, Juvenile Hedgehogs, Bats: St Tiggy-winkles glop

Seed-eating Birds: Foreign finch mix, British finch mix, any wild seeds

Insect-eating Birds: white clean maggots, natural pinkies, natural squats (available from angling shops), mealworms

Pigeons, Doves: Complan (for babies), mixed corn

Kingfishers, Grebes, Diving (fish-eating) Ducks: Whitebait

Dabbling (surface feeding) Ducks: chick crumbs (for babies), mixed corn

Herons, Seabirds: sprats, frozen day-old chicks

Swans, Geese: mixed corn, bread on water

Birds of Prey, Foxes, Badgers, Mustelids, Corvids: frozen day-old chicks, frozen mice

Deer, Rabbits, Hares: coarse goat mix, dandelion leaves

Mice, Voles: dry porridge oats, apple

Bats: glop, natural pinkies, small mealworms

Water voles, Glis glis: apples

Lizards, Frogs, Toads: natural pinkies

Squirrels: peanuts in shell

Most Baby Mammals: unpasteurised goats' milk

In all cases the first day's fluid should be Lectade

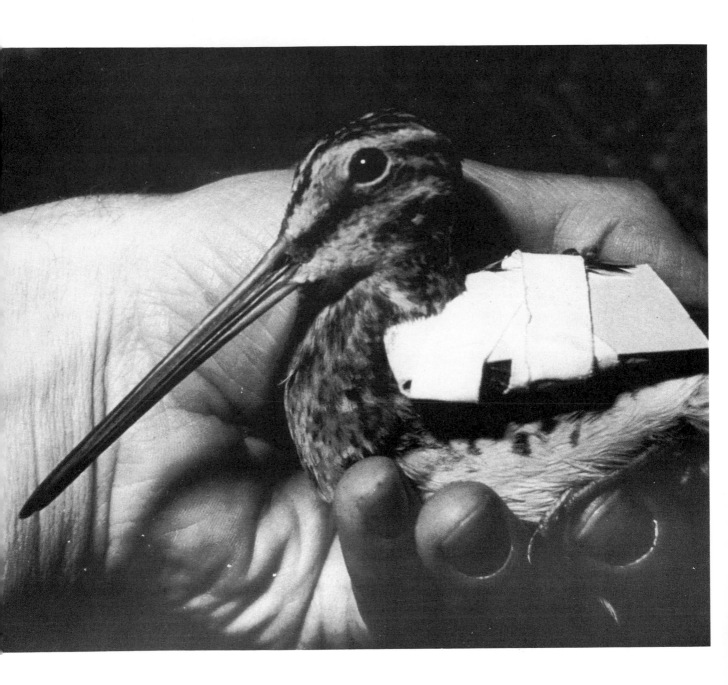

RECIPE FOR ST TIGGYWINKLES GLOP

Suitable for bats, raising some baby birds, and weaning hedgehogs and other small meat-eating mammals:

Cup Pedigree Chum puppy food
Cup dried insect food
   (Sluis Universal or Haiths Prosecto)
Cup cold water
5cm high calorie vitamin concentrate
   (8 in 1 Pet Products Inc.)
¼ teaspoon bone meal feed
¼ teaspoon Can-Addase enzyme
   (available through vets)

Liquidise till smooth and the consistency of soft ice cream. Should be discarded after twenty-four hours.

simply wither away. That was until one particular snipe, a small wader with a ridiculously long beak, totally ignored all the offerings in the aquarium and looked doomed to disaster. Our garden is constantly damp under-foot – the whole of Aylesbury must be built on a bog, judging by the state of the ground after a wet winter. Damp, muddy ground is ideal for earthworms, white worms and other subterranean creepy-crawlies. I knew that each time I turned the soil over in the aviaries there was a wriggling mass of superb wader food. In desperation I let the doomed snipe go in the small bird aviary. Within minutes he was pushing into the

An injured snipe.

soft soil, time and again pulling out and swallowing tiny creatures. The aviary was shared with a few blackbirds and a mistle thrush. The thrush had the really charming habit of emptying their bowl of maggots in every direction, and as I watched the snipe's antics, from the kitchen window, I even saw him pick up some of the itinerant maggots.

About a week later Jenny Babb, the Trust's membership secretary, brought over in a cardboard box what was supposedly another snipe casualty. As I slid my hand into the box and steadied the bird I knew at once that it was not a snipe. It was a woodcock, a much larger wader, for some reason prized as a target by the shooting fraternity. I lifted the woodcock out, showing Sarah, Jenny's young daughter, how its large eyes were mounted so that it could see backwards as well as forwards, a remarkable adaptation for sitting motionless and virtually invisible in leaf litter in deciduous woodland.

I could see no obvious injury but as I held the bird I could feel an ominous bubbling in its chest: moist râles that signified pneumonia, aspergillus (a fungus infecting the lungs), or something worse. Obviously the bird's condition had reduced it to a state where it could be picked up – a sure sign of its imminent demise. As usual there were no guidelines on how to treat a woodock so I jumped in with both feet, starting a course of antibiotics and giving it minute doses of Lasix, a diuretic we had previously used on mammals.

For the time being I put the woodcock into

one of the heated intensive care cages, which already held some much smaller birds. At the time the other heated cages were fully occupied: some held pigeons, which are much larger than a woodcock, and one contained only a concussed great spotted woodpecker which could become very aggressive to other birds put in with her.

Unfortunately the woodcock, with his great legs and massive feet, kept treading on the smaller birds as he marched up and down, and he also knocked over his dish of maggots three times, scattering potential greenbottles to every corner of the cage. This was another desperate case, and so once again I resorted to using the outside aviary. Placing the woodcock here, I hoped he would emulate the snipe's feeding propensity. All through that evening and night I kept checking his progress, fully expecting him to be dead by the morning. However he wasn't: he was trundling up and down, probing just like the snipe. So far so good.

I allowed him two days to settle and then caught him so that I could dose him with thiabendazole. This was in case the moist râles were caused by the tracheal parasitic worm *Syngamus*. With most birds it's possible to probe the trachea with a swab and get a sample of exuded matter so that the parasite can be identified. However, because of the tube-like nature and small gape of a woodcock's beak it is impossible to carry out this simple diagnostic procedure.

Les with the newly arrived woodcock.

There is also a major problem in trying to give drugs orally, especially thiabendazole. After a few attempts I eventually succeeded by turning the unfortunate woodcock completely upside down and slowly trickling the wormer along the roof of his mouth so that the liquid could not enter his trachea and drown him.

The two waders, Captain Beaky the snipe and Splinter the woodcock, thrived in each other's company. Both much recovered, they could be seen from the kitchen window marching up and down as they endlessly probed for food morsels, with the woodcock in front and the snipe, not unlike a miniature version of his leader, taking up the rear.

You may have noticed, if you have followed the progress of the Hospital, that we are constantly reviewing our use of drugs and consequently are introducing more and more sophisticated treatments for previously untreated conditions. In the case of the woodcock, we were able to adapt the use of two drugs to treat his specific conditions.

There are so few groups in the country with a professional attitude to the care of wild animals and birds that the media do seem to visit us at least twice each week for newspaper or television pictures. True the coverage does generate more casualties, but this is good news – it means that more people become aware of the worth of saving wildlife casualties, and of course that more of the casualties can receive proper treatment.

During those early mild months in 1989 we were inundated with all forms of media interest, and Sue volunteered me (alone) for the early morning breakfast shows.

In one week I was driving out of Aylesbury every day before dawn to go to some studio or other. I even shared a programme in Birmingham with a non-hibernating seven-spotted ladybird which had been chauffeured down from Preston.

All the British television channels, including the cable network, carried items on the Trust. American, French and German crews made the pilgrimage to Aylesbury. So did the Reuters man, as well as all the national newspapers. On Monday 13th February our work with hedgehogs was shown on seven consecutive national news programmes. The post resulting from this is still coming in, after the Post Office have managed to sort out all the crazy addresses. People knock the Post Office, but the way they have handled this avalanche of incorrectly addressed mail has been marvellous. Our local postman is now always snowed under with letters for us. He has found it amusing to try and decipher the addresses – and, I must add, to ring our clamorous doorbell at seven o'clock in the morning on the 16th just to tell us it was snowing. I appreciated that.

It all seems a long way from my first encounter with hedgehogs at Harrods and on the golf course at New Malden, which I wrote about in *The Complete Hedgehog*. More than any other animals, hedgehogs have been a great part of my life and threaten to take over.

Why I should have fallen for hedgehogs in a big way remains a mystery. They are grumpy little creatures who when you first meet them will try to spike you, or at best will attempt to trap an unwary finger by curling into a ball. As they start to feel better at the Hospital the hedgehogs take on their own individual characters. Just looking at the names on their record cards gives the newcomer an inkling of what may be lurking within a few of the cages. There have, of course, been 'Jaws' and 'Fang', and the latest terror is 'Watch it', but the real hoax is little 'Snuggles'. Sounds cosy, doesn't it? Snuggles came in having been treated by a vet for a chest infection. I had my doubts and unrolled him just in case. It was just as well I did, for in fact his throat had been cut by lethal plastic netting. I routinely cleaned the wound and – just my luck – found a fractured artery which proceeded to squirt blood everywhere. At times like that you panic. The artery was no thicker than a piece of cotton but I managed to clamp it and tie it off with catgut. Snuggles also had a badly infected shoulder which, although a lot better, still impairs the use of one of his front legs. However, nothing impairs his jaws, and now – can you blame him? – as you pick him up you are confronted with a swaying head with a set of teeth that will clamp onto anything within the arc of attack. Many a new volunteer cleaning out the intensive care unit has made the

Patches can only manage half a roll.

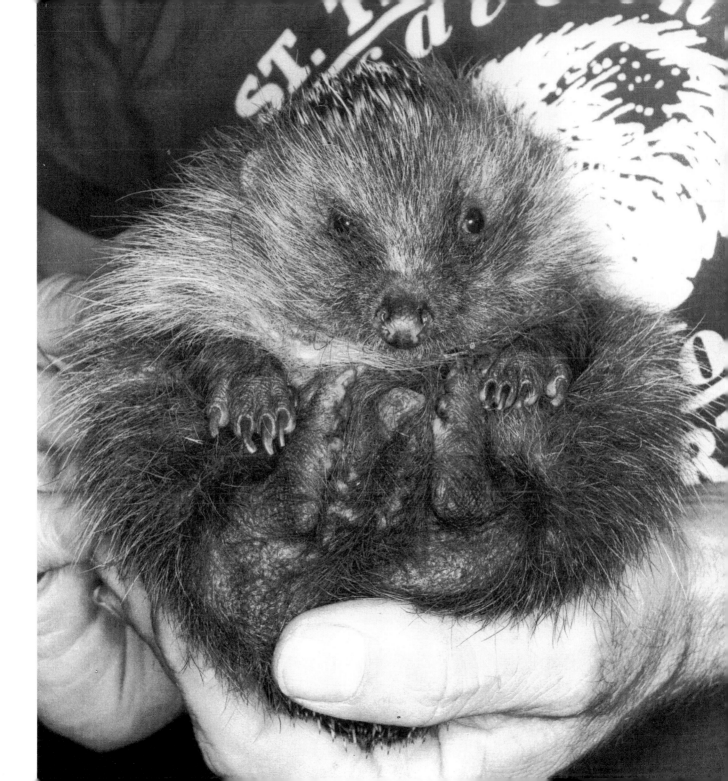

Curly and Patches.

painful mistake of trying to cuddle the cutely-named Snuggles.

Patches was so-named because it was such a huge job to stitch him up. I have now had the privilege of Patches's company for over two years. This does not mean that I advocate keep-ing hedgehogs as pets for they do not take kindly to captivity. Although he lives with us, Patches still leads a full life and regularly meets other hedgehogs passing through the Hospital and has helped many overcome the trauma of their early confinement.

At the time of his accident Patches lost a wide strip of skin down one side. Since then he has never been able to again master the supreme hedgehog ploy of rolling into a ball. If you touch his nose (avoiding getting bitten), he will try to roll but only gets halfway, leaving his legs flailing hopelessly in the air. In the wild he would have no defence against many of the hazards and predators to which evolution has made the hedgehog invincible to.

Hedgehogs are not all the cute little animals we imagine them to be. Every now and then there is a Rambo who likes nothing better than to snort at or fight its room-mates. Each cage had to regularly be listened to and watched for bullying of any of the more vulnerable patients. The most vulnerable, and also the most noisily aggressive, is the female hedgehog called Curly. As soon as Curly meets another hedgehog she snorts and charges, which is all very well and natural until you realise that Curly is practically devoid of spines, the first line of defence against even other hedgehogs.

She came into us in 1988, a weak shivering tiny mite who possessed just one or two spines. Her bald skin was in an appalling condition, a battlefield between fleas, ticks, mites and ringworm. We treated her with warm Alugan baths and gradually the infestation receded until we had a tiny hedgehog, as bald as an egg but with shiny healthy skin. As hedgehog spines provide insulation as well as defence, Curly lived her first few months with us under a heat-lamp in intensive care.

Gradually little pins pricked through her skin as her new crop of spines started to grow. There were only a few but we hoped more would follow. But they never did and even these existing spines grew twisted and curled over, completely useless to a hedgehog but a good lead for a name. Her problem appears to be genetic and not only should she not be released in this condition, but also we would be irresponsible if we let her breed in captivity. However, being a hedgehog she in no way minds being kept in solitary confinement provided she has constant warmth and bowls of dog food.

I could go on about hedgehogs for ever. Every one that comes in is a character with many of our resident stars like Snowflake, Patches, Curly and Earthquake known the world over. Even St Tiggywinkles seems now to be a household name.

St Tiggywinkles started out as a shed rescue centre for hedgehogs but it is now to become Britain's first purpose-built teaching hospital to treat all species of wild animals. And they say, 'What's in a name?'

12 Owls, Cubs and Twins

Whatever happens to be inside the cardboard boxes brought to our door, it never fails to fascinate me. The title of my previous book, *Something in a Cardboard Box*, perfectly describes our way of life at the Hospital and, of course, on publication brought the inevitable question from an interviewer: 'Do you have at the moment any unusual animal which came to you in a cardboard box?'

I replied that as we were reasonably slack at that time of year there was not the huge influx of casualties we would expect in the summer months.

Why didn't I keep my big mouth firmly closed? Whenever I remark on there being a lack of incoming patients they seem to start flooding in again, and they are not always welcome. When I say 'not welcome' it's not that I resent any animal arriving. It's just that sometimes the circumstances of its predicament could have been avoided with just a modicum of thought. This is especially true when captive-bred, non-indigenous animals escape into the totally alien British countryside and then arrive on my doorstep because they are not fully

equipped to survive in the wild.

One particular cardboard box turned up just two days prior to the launch of the book. It was supposed to contain a long-eared owl, which, though feasible, was most unusual from the urban sprawl of Hemel Hempstead. I am quite used to handling all the British species of owl and generally prefer not to use gloves, as I then have much better control of their wings and their talons. Before fully opening the lid of the cardboard box, which usually causes the bird to panic at the sudden influx of light, I normally quietly slip my hand in and control the bird. This long-eared owl would not be a problem to hold – the long-eared is a much easier bird to handle than the tawny owl, which at 38 centimetres in length is slightly the larger of the two species.

Carefully I slid my hand under the flap but stopped as soon as I felt this owl's head touching the top of the box. The box was 60 centimetres high. This was a very large long-eared owl. I reached down and felt its massive shoulders, and then, since discretion is the better part of valour, hastily withdrew my now obviously vulnerable hand and firmly closed the monster inside its box.

Sensibly armoured with double thick welder's gloves I once more approached the box and gingerly lifted one of the lid flaps. Two enormous orange eyes blinked up at me from beneath two long feather tufts. These were the 'long ears' of the British species, but this bird was much, much larger than any owl found in Britain (other than the two male snowy owls on Fetlar in the Shetlands, which were not likely to be seen in this part of the country). Then it dawned on me. This was no long-eared owl – it was an eagle owl, one of the largest species of owl in the world. This giant bird lived on young roe deer or foxes, and was a daunting prospect by any twist of the imagination.

It was not the time for finesse as I grabbed him with my cumbersome welder's gloves. He came out of the box a clucking, furious mass of beak and feathers with wings that filled our reception area. I had him under control, I think. My immediate assumption was that he had escaped from captivity – and my reference books later confirmed that no eagle owl had been recorded wild in this country for over eighty years, although they are not uncommon in other parts of northern Europe.

With a little detective work my assumption was proved correct – his primary feathers and wing tips showed considerable damage, the result of trying to fly in an inadequate aviary. At the Hospital we did not have a cage large enough to house such a huge owl, and so for the moment I moved a fox out of the dog pen, put in some perches and installed 'Bubo' there.

The questions that arose were: 'Where did the bird come from?' and 'Who owned it and let it go?' It had no rings or obvious distinguishing marks. In fact it looked just like any other eagle owl. It seemed a good idea to get details of the owl's plight published in as many places as possible, together with a request for the owner

to get in touch with us. While we were at it we added the proviso that its former quarters should be inspected to see if they were truly suitable to house such a large bird again.

Sounds simple, doesn't it? The newspapers and television companies obliged and soon Bubo's predicament was known throughout Britain. But then the deluge started. As Sue put it, 'Everybody and his mother seemed to have lost an eagle owl.' There were dozens of claimants who had lost eagle owls from as far afield as Dover and Bristol. I hate to think just how many of these giant birds were flying around Britain, preying, no doubt, on rabbits, hedgehogs and the occasional cat. Now we had to ask for written claims, preferably with a photograph or other proof of ownership.

In the midst of all the hubbub of the owl, its claimants, the media and the launch of my new book, we had to deal with the influx of casualty calls I had invited with my rash statement that business was slack. I even took an emergency call which caused me to break off in the middle of a radio interview and set out, hotfoot, for Chalfont St Giles, over 30 kilometres away.

The call from Chiltern Open Air Museum described how a pile of timber had been moved, revealing three badger cubs; these had been promptly picked up and deposited in the museum office. There seemed to be some reluctance to stop moving the timber, and so I arranged to rendezvous at the site with an RSPCA

The eagle owl was a daunting prospect.

The artificial fox den made from 'rotten old timber'.

inspector, in case the weight of the badger protection laws had to be brought to bear.

My first task on arrival was to assess the age and stage of the badger cubs, really to give us time to decide what action to take. As far as I knew nobody had ever tried to replace badger cubs once their sett had been disturbed, and so there were no recommended procedures. There was simply our own initiative.

In the office I quietly approached the box of hay and gingerly pushed it aside, fully expecting to see and hear three little pink and black striped heads. However, the three brown heads that mewed at my intrusion were definitely not badger cubs – they were fox cubs. This was going to make our task much easier, as I had on numerous occasions successfully reunited fox cubs with their mothers.

The pile of enormous black timbers had not been completely dismantled; clambering in, we started to fashion a sort of enclosure for the fox cubs from some of the smaller timbers. Much of the wood was rotting and easy to break into the lengths required to make a wall that would be both cub-proof and low enough for the vixen to get over. We were kicking and banging the timbers into shape when somebody spotted a nearly black vixen, sitting looking at us from no more than 15 metres away. We decided to put the cubs into the enclosure and withdraw.

She was obviously waiting for us to leave, but just to make sure we asked the museum staff to check the following morning that she had moved the cubs. We asked them not to move any more timbers without making sure the site had been vacated. In fact, I suggested that it would be a good idea to leave all that rotten old timber lying as a catacombed refuge for wildlife. 'That rotten timber,' insisted the Curator, 'is in fact a fourteenth-century tithe barn which we are going to reassemble provided we can replace the broken lengths.'

As they say in the comic strips, 'Gulp!' Feeling like desecrators of a holy building, we left along the muddy track as fast as I could drive.

The cubs were moved by the vixen, their rightful guardian, but the continuing saga of the eagle owl looked like never coming to a satisfactory conclusion, although we were receiving all manner of letters, threats and photographs. We finally settled for the woman from Hemel Hempstead whose photographs, although not spot on, were near enough to Bubo to satisfy all of us, and so we allowed her to come and collect him.

In the lulls between all the media commotions, the clicking of newspaper cameramen and the banging of television clapper-boards, a curious 'whickering' noise could be heard emanating from our corner shed. We all knew what it was but did not want the outside world to know of the little miracle which had recently occurred at our Hospital. All the visitors accepted that it was common-or-garden tawny owls squabbling, and luckily nobody asked to see them.

I had first noticed minuscule 'whickering' sounds coming from the large wire-topped box which we call 'the Coffin'. We use it to restrict badger and deer that have orthopaedic injuries and need close confinement for a while. In occupation at that time was Beatty, a female badger, the victim of the inevitable road traffic accident. On arrival the bruising around her pelvis spelled trouble in a female as any injury could impair her cub-bearing potential. However an X-ray showed her pelvis to be intact, although her left hip joint was dislocated with the leg hanging uselessly. Manipulation of her other

Beattie with her dislocated hip strapped up.

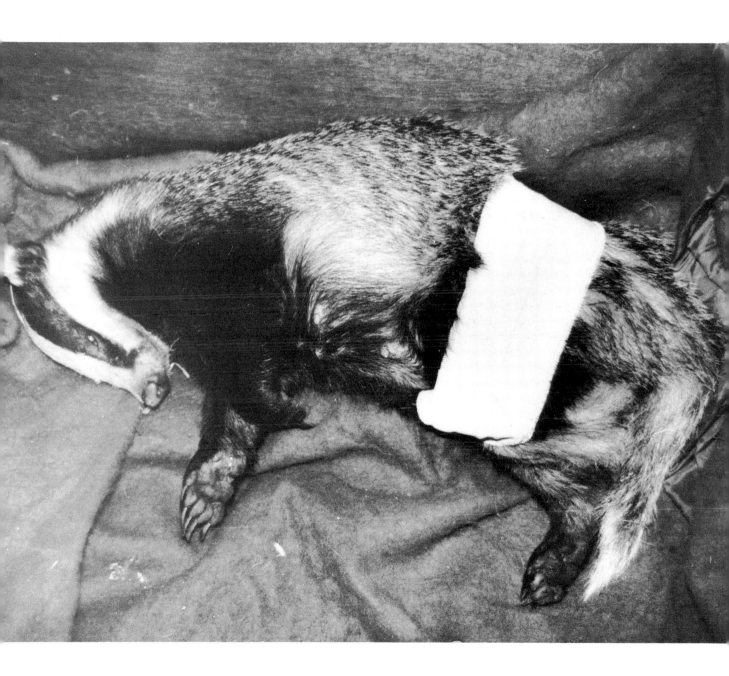

hind leg pointed to a snapped cruciate ligament, making that leg as useless as the other.

The ligament operation could wait, so under anaesthetic we first relocated the hip joint and then strapped the whole of her left leg to her body with yards of adhesive plaster wrapped around her middle.

After a week we once again anaesthetised Beatty, this time to remove the strapping – her own muscles would now hold the leg in place. While she was unconscious we took the opportunity to operate on the damaged cruciate ligament. I marvelled at the vet's dexterity in operating to help this badger walk again – somehow when a good surgeon cuts into an animal it's not the bloody mess you would expect to see, so please bear with me.

With the hock joint exposed he calmly drilled a hole in each of the bones normally joined by the ligament. Then the marvel: cutting a narrow strip of skin from the incision site, he threaded it through the opposing holes and firmly stitched each end to the powerful muscle fibres of the badger's leg, creating an artificial tendon which he informed me would be functional while Beatty's own body produced its own substitute. This is apparently an operation commonly performed on dogs and cats, but, although we had performed this operation on the dog fox, once again I am sure that it was the first time it had been performed on a badger.

Slowly over the next few weeks of necessary confinement, Beatty began to regain the use of her legs. It was during this period of physiotherapy that I noticed Beatty's teats becoming enlarged. And then one day, the 25th February to be precise, on going out of the back door for my early morning round, I heard a new noise. It was not any of my patients, for I knew all their calls intimately. This was a new sound, a tiny peeping, obviously out of tune with the familiar sounds of the Hospital. Like an owl I followed it with my ears, gradually tracking it down to the confines of 'the Coffin'. Then I knew what had happened as, ever so silently, I lifted the cover. In the half light I could just make out Beatty nuzzling a little pink sausage, a newly born badger cub. Another tiny brother or sister groped blindly under Beatty's tummy; that epitome of fierceness the badger was now lying on her side, a big cuddly mum. She sensed I was there and leapt to her feet, leaving her babies twittering. In a flash I had the cover back on and tiptoed to the kitchen to shout for Sue so that I could tell her the great news.

For the next three days that end of the garden was off-limits to everybody. I did not know whether badger mums were like hedgehog mums and would harm their young. I was not taking any chances and for the moment only went to the Coffin to replenish Beatty's water and food bowls.

Every day I listened for the now familiar twittering. All seemed well, Beatty was eating and any time I caught a glimpse of her babies they seemed healthy and robust.

New-born badger cubs, February 25th 1989.

Then disaster struck. The good old British weather, which had been so mild, suddenly turned freezing. I covered the Coffin with blankets, but on the morning after the first severe frost all was quiet. Frantically I peeped into the nursery. There was no sign of life as Beatty had pulled all the bedding over the top of them. Then a faint twitter emanated from the depths of the hay. This was a relief for the moment, but I realised I would have to make other arrangements and run the risk of moving the little family to warmer quarters.

The corner shed would be ideal. It was a reasonably new structure and was only used to store cages and gardening tools. I had one of my purges and threw a lot of old stuff away. Isn't it funny that when you have to find space you suddenly realise that all the stuff you have been hoarding is just junk that you will never ever use?

I had to line the bottom of the shed with stout timber for in spite of her softness as a mother Beatty was still a badger and quite capable of breaking out of any shed that wasn't specially reinforced. I installed a heat lamp, and then, with the addition of a large bundle of hay, the new nursery was ready for occupation. This was the traumatic moment. I knew that I would have to move Beatty across with the grasper, not knowing whether this would completely turn her off motherhood.

I reached into the Coffin, trying to grasp her without endangering the cubs. She cried out, but the badgers had to be moved, and it was only an instant until she was in the hay of her new home. I put on gloves to pick up the cubs, still in their bedding. I did not want to put my scent on the little badgers. Deftly, I put them into the new nursery and quickly closed the door to let Beatty settle and hopefully pick up where she had left off.

For three nail-biting hours I waited before looking in again. I had taken the risk that she might reject the cubs and that I would have to hand rear them, though with the Coffin so exposed I had really had no choice in the matter. As quietly as possible I turned the key, so intent that I did not notice until too late the enormous 'swan-pat' I was treading in. A female swan with us at that time had the habit of squatting in the corner in front of the shed and leaving enormous quantities of guano – as only swans can – to trap any unwary foot.

Ignoring the mess over my shoe, I peered into the darkness, turned the light quickly on and then off but with enough time to see Beatty lying there with her two little cubs, now faintly striped on their heads, firmly glued to her tummy, paws paddling. All was well, though the stress was just like becoming a father again.

Beatty and her cubs continued to grow during all the commotion of the eagle owl and the reconstruction work on the next door veterinary unit. Her two cubs, as yet with no names, are starting to look like badgers, and their eyes are just opening to take a first look at the big

The cubs' eyes began to open at about five weeks.

world there inside the shed.

It's so much easier when the natural mother rears her own young. Our baby season has just started with the annual influx of orphans. This second weekend in April has seen the arrival of two young blackbirds and a baby rabbit caught by cats, two nestlings of unidentifiable species, a really tiny pigeon named Walter and, the most endearing of all, a muntjac fawn named Dotty Dearest, whose mother was shot, and a baby hare named Kenny Leveret – his mother was torn apart by dogs. I am sorry to leave you on a note of such conflicting emotions but such is the nature of wildlife care – one minute you are up and the next minute you are kicked in the teeth. Yet it is still better than it used to be, and is now so important in people's minds that the future for the wild casualty looks extremely rosy.

LEFT *Tiny Dotty Dearest in the incubator.*

Postscript 1990/91

The good news is that our dream of Europe's first wildlife teaching hospital is now almost a reality in a conservation partnership with Buckinghamshire County Council on land in the Aylesbury area. This momentous step and our positive attitude to saving wild animals and birds have already encouraged many others to take up the gauntlet. At last rescue centres are springing up all over Britain as well as in Australia, South America and Africa; in North America, New Zealand and parts of Europe such centres are already well established.

It is you, our friends and supporters, who have made all this possible. Together with our tremendous volunteer workforce and perennial supporters like BP, British Telecom, Legal and General, Oral B and now Rolex, you have made the dream a reality.

Edmund Burke once said that nobody made a greater mistake than he who did nothing because he could only do a little.

Saving wild animals and birds used to be something which was done only 'a little' but now it is a major factor in protecting all our futures.

Of course, we still need support for the maintenance of our ever-increasing flock of patients, so if you feel like helping with our project please contact us at:

St Tiggywinkles Wildlife Teaching Hospital
Enquiries HF
Aylesbury
Bucks HP21 7NY
England

ALSO AVAILABLE FROM CHATTO & WINDUS

0 7011 3272 8	THE COMPLETE HEDGEHOG	LES STOCKER	£8.99
0 7011 3500 X	THE COMPLETE BAT	JAMES ROBERTSON	£8.99
0 7011 3329 5	SOMETHING IN A CARDBOARD BOX	LES STOCKER	£8.95
0 7011 3402 X	OPERATION OTTER	PHILIP WAYRE	£8.95
0 7011 3456 9	THE FLOWERING OF BRITAIN	RICHARD MABEY and TONY EVANS	£10.95

All these books are available at your bookshop or can be ordered from the following address:

Chatto & Windus
Cash Sales Department
P.O. Box 11, Falmouth,
Cornwall TR10 9EN

Please send a cheque or postal order (no currency) and allow 60p for postage and packing for the first book plus 25p for the second book and 15p for each additional book ordered up to a maximum charge of £1.90 in UK.

B.F.P.O. customers please allow 60p for the first book, 25p for the second book plus 15p per copy for the next 7 books, thereafter 9p per book.

Overseas customers, including Eire, please allow £1.25 for postage and packing for the first book, 75p for the second book, and 28p for each subsequent title ordered.

The prices shown above were correct at the time of going to press. However Chatto & Windus reserve the right to show new retail prices on covers which may differ from those previously advertised in the text or elsewhere.